Tamara gave him a sexy smile. "To be honest, I'm not sleepy at all. I'm in the mood for another movie. What about you? You think you can stay up long enough to watch one?"

Micah got into bed with her. "I can't believe that you're still talking trash. You'll be the first one to fall asleep."

She laughed. "You're sure I'm not keeping you up, old man?" Tamara asked.

"I got your old man."

Tamara wrapped her arms around him, pulling him closer to her. She could feel his uneven breathing on her cheek as he held her tightly.

Micah traced his fingertip across her lip, causing Tamara's skin to tingle. He paused to kiss her, sending currents of desire through her.

She caressed the strong tendons in the back of his neck.

"Make love to me," Tamara whispered between kisses. She was ready to take their relationship to the next level.

"You don't know how badly I've wanted to hear those words come out of your mouth," Micah confessed.

Books by Jacquelin Thomas

Kimani Romance

The Pastor's Woman
Teach Me Tonight

JACQUELIN THOMAS

is the bestselling author of more than thirty books and is an avid reader of romance novels when she's not writing. She and her family live in North Carolina, where she is busy working on her next project.

Teach Me Tonight
Jacquelin Thomas

HOLLINGTON HOMECOMING
Where old friends reunite...and new passions take flight

To my wonderful Husband…just because…

Special thanks and acknowledgment to Jacquelin Thomas for her contribution to the Hollington Homecoming miniseries.

KIMANI PRESS™

ISBN-13: 978-0-373-86133-0

Recycling programs for this product may not exist in your area.

TEACH ME TONIGHT

www.kimanipress.com

Printed in U.S.A.

Dear Reader,

I really enjoyed writing *Teach Me Tonight* and getting to know the characters. What's really special about this story is that I have two grandchildren whose names are Micah and Tamara. Memories of my college days were prominent in my mind during the writing of this story. I was moved to reconnect with some of my old friends from school and found that one of my dearest friends had passed on. She'd crossed my mind many times over the years, but life just got in the way and I never followed through with contacting her. I challenge each of you not to let another day go by without picking up the phone or e-mailing someone you haven't spoken to in a while.

Settle down with your favorite coffee or cup of tea and prepare to get to know Micah and Tamara. Don't forget to enjoy the Homecoming weekend. GO LIONS!

As always, I thank you for your support.

Jacquelin

Chapter 1

"The wedding ring is the outward and visible sign of an inward and spiritual bond that unites two loyal hearts in endless love."

Tamara Hodges smiled through tears as she relieved her sister Callie of the enormous wedding bouquet she had insisted on carrying down the aisle.

"It is a seal of the vows Bryant and Callie have made to one another."

She wiped her eyes with a lace handkerchief as she witnessed the exchange of rings between her baby sister and new brother-in-law, wishing them love and happiness for the rest of their lives.

Tamara's thoughts traveled to the one person she kept hidden in her heart—the one man she could never forget. The one person with whom she dreamed of sharing that type of love.

The pastor's words drew her attention back to the ceremony.

"You may now kiss your bride."

Tamara stole a quick peek at her mother, who was seated in the front row, fighting back tears.

Three hundred guests erupted in applause as Mr. and Mrs. Bryant Charles Madison were introduced. The music began, prompting the newlyweds to lead the recessional from the sanctuary.

As Bryant's best man escorted her down the aisle, Tamara could feel her ex-stepfather's heated glare as she strolled past him, her head held up high. She refused to let him put a damper on her blissful mood.

Outside the sanctuary, Tamara and Callie embraced.

"Congratulations," she whispered as she gazed into a pair of hazel-green eyes that mirrored her own. "I'm so happy for you, Callie."

Tamara embraced Bryant next. "I guess we're stuck with you now."

"Yeah," he replied, giving his new wife a sidelong glance. "Because I'm not going anywhere. I love this girl."

"Good," Tamara said with a smile. "That's what I want to hear."

Wedding guests filed out of the church, each one pausing to congratulate the bride and groom.

Tamara's mother walked up and said, "The ceremony was beautiful, wasn't it?"

She nodded. "Yeah, it was."

When Lucas, her ex-stepfather entered into the

church foyer, Tamara uttered, "We should go back into the sanctuary. It's time for pictures."

Her mother agreed.

Just being in that man's presence stirred up shadows and fears that made her uncomfortable. Tamara did not want to mar Callie's wedding day, so she decided to stay as far away from Lucas as possible.

After the traditional wedding-party photos, a limo whisked them to the Four Seasons Hotel Atlanta for the reception. Callie and Bryant were in a separate stretch limo, which followed close behind.

Her mother suggested that the photographer shoot some pictures on the grand staircase at the hotel, saying that the brass railing would serve as the perfect backdrop. She had even arranged to have the large floral centerpiece at the foot of the staircase coordinate with the wedding colors and flowers. Whatever Jillian Hodges-Devane wanted she got.

Tamara made small talk with the other members of the bridal party during the ride over to the midtown hotel.

The ballroom where the reception was held consisted of a wall of mirrors on one end highlighted by large crystal chandeliers and large picture windows at the other. Tamara had been in the same room a week ago, covering an event for *Luster* magazine.

She enjoyed writing for the magazine but had dreams of starting her own publication one day.

The wedding party waited in line outside as they waited to be announced. The best man again escorted Tamara into the ballroom. After the wedding party, Mr. and Mrs. Bryant Charles Madison made their grand entrance.

While waiters navigated about the room carrying

trays of hors d' oeuvres, Tamara mingled, pausing to speak to relatives and friends of her family. She felt the sensation that someone was watching her and turned; meeting her ex-stepfather's dark and insolent gaze, she straightened herself with dignity.

He smirked, gave a slight nod and then turned his attention back to his daughter, Callie.

Tamara's eyes bounced around the room, looking for her mother.

"How are you holding up, Mama?" she asked when she found her seated at one of the family tables. Tamara sat down in the empty chair beside her.

"I'm exhausted," Jillian responded. "Your sister looks lovely, doesn't she?"

Tamara agreed. "And very happy. I guess all the whining, fussing and craziness she put us through over the past year has been worth it. I'm so glad that girl is married."

"Seeing Callie and Bryant like this—it was definitely worth it," her mother responded. "One day we'll be doing this for you. Hopefully, it will happen while I'm still young enough to enjoy the wedding."

Tamara drew an invisible pattern on the tablecloth. "Don't hold your breath, Mama. I'd actually have to have a man in my life in order to get married."

"So there's no one special? You haven't met anyone?"

"Mama, have you considered that I might be one of those women who are destined to remain single?"

"Bite your tongue," Jillian stated. "Don't even put that thought in your head. A beautiful woman like you won't have a problem finding a husband. You only have to open your heart and allow him entry."

Tamara caught her mother looking at her ex-stepfather. "Mama…"

"Can you believe he had the nerve to bring that woman here? She is what—barely legal? Lucas Devane always had an eye for young girls." Rancor sharpened Jillian's voice.

"To be honest with you, I don't really care enough about him to even wonder," Tamara retorted.

Her mother leaned over and embraced her. "I love you, Tammy. I hope you know that."

"Mama, I know you do. I love you, too," Tamara assured her. "We all went through a bad time, but thank God that it's over now. Oh, could you please just call me Tamara?" Her eyes traveled back over to the table where Lucas sat with his girlfriend. "I'm not Tammy anymore, so please don't call me that."

Lucas's eyes met hers, and his lips turned into a cynical smile. Tamara's eyes never wavered as she stared him down until he had the good sense to drop his gaze.

"I hate him," her mother uttered. A sudden thin chill hung on the edge of her words.

"I don't have any feelings toward him at all," Tamara stated. "Lucas could drop dead right here in the middle of the room and it wouldn't phase me at all." She turned her attention back to Callie and Bryant, her thoughts roaming once more to the one and only love of her life.

Micah Ross.

He was definitely the one who got away, Tamara decided. She had allowed her fears and insecurities of her youth to keep her from opening up completely and trusting, which caused Tamara to push him away. Micah had always been nothing less than a good friend to her and her math tutor, but because of her inability to trust combined with a group of immature boys who had nothing better to do other than playing pranks, she treated him cruelly the night of their graduation from Hollington College.

She pushed away from the table and helped herself to the caramelized Vidalia onion tart with goat cheese, lobster and chive risotto fritters and miniature crab cake hors d'oeuvres.

Jillian rose to her feet and followed her daughter. "I was thinking… Isn't Bryant's best man single? I heard that he's the vice president of Atlanta Bank and Trust."

"Not interested, Mama," Tamara said in a low voice. "Now just drop it."

She released a short sigh of relief when her mother became distracted by relatives. This would give Tamara a break from her constant matchmaking.

Twenty minutes later, everyone was seated. They dined on a duo entrée of tenderloin of beef and salmon, roasted potatoes, asparagus and béarnaise sauce while the band, which was personally selected by Jillian, played softly in the background.

"Mama was right about the menu," Callie whispered to her. "This was the perfect choice."

Tamara agreed. She sliced off a piece of the tender salmon and stuck it into her mouth, remembering the argument between her mother and sister over the food for the reception. They ended up not talking for two days.

Callie won the fight between them over the wedding cake. Her mother, a true Southern lady, wanted the butter pecan cake with a fresh peach filling while her sister insisted on the Tahitian vanilla butter cake, Tahitian vanilla custard and fresh berries.

Tamara left the reception shortly after her sister's departure and headed home. After she changed out of the bridesmaid gown, Tamara settled down on the chaise in her bedroom to write in her journal.

August 22

My sister married her high-school sweetheart today. It was a beautiful wedding, making it hard not to wonder if I'll ever have one of my own. I have not been able to have a relationship any longer than six or seven months. As I get older, I find that I'm able to detect the lies much quicker.

If I am to be completely honest, then I must admit that part of the reason I haven't found my Mr. Right is because I treated him horribly when we were in college.

Right before graduation, I overheard some boys saying that Micah was planning on having sex with me and that he was going to play the "you're the love of my life" card because that's what it would take to get me into bed.

I don't know why I believed them, but graduation night, when he told me that he loved me, I told him that I would never date a man like him and basically that he wasn't good enough for me. It wasn't until much later that I realized Micah didn't say those things—the guys had been joking around and knew that I was listening to the conversation.

I want to explain but Micah never returned my

phone calls, and the next thing I knew he had moved to Los Angeles.

Our ten-year college reunion and homecoming is coming up in October, but I'm not sure if Micah will be coming. I hope that he will be in attendance…. I want to try and talk to him one more time.

He is a famous record mogul now, but I don't care about that. I just want a chance to apologize to Micah. The tabloids have him romantically involved with that model Sunni, so it is not as if he is available anyway. The truth is that I really miss his friendship.

I miss him.

Los Angeles, California

Micah Ross stepped out of the sleek black limo in the midst of a sea of hungry media photographers and reporters. He focused his attention on the door of the Wilshire Grand Hotel several yards away while assisting his date out of the car.

He hated all the attention on him, but Micah knew that it was an integral part of his business. He was the man who had turned a tiny music store into million-dollar record label Ross Red. His first two records sold a combined 1.5 million copies before the mainstream music industry knew he existed. Now his $500 million empire included music, clothes, real estate, a product line of computers and communications.

A musician himself, Micah believed that one could only go so far in the music business—something he tried to drill into all of his artists. He pushed to get them to understand that they needed to acquire the necessary skills and education to have other options because one never knew what was going to go up and what would go down.

"Over here, Mr. Ross," a photographer shouted.

Micah glanced in his direction and pasted on a smile. His mouth tightened as Sunni, a supermodel, wrapped her arms around him as cameras flashed all around them.

"Micah, please smile," she whispered. "At least try to look like you're enjoying my company."

He chuckled. "Sunni, you know that I always enjoy hanging out with you."

"Then smile. Just remember that you're the man they all want to be. You are one of the most influential and wealthiest men in the world, Micah. Baby, you should flaunt it."

All Micah wanted to do was get inside the hotel. He hated walking the red carpet and avoided it whenever he could. Of course, in his business one needed the media to be successful.

Grinning, Sunni posed for more photos along the red carpet. She loved the spotlight so much so that it was rumored she called or texted photographers her itinerary from time to time.

Once inside, they were still under the microscope as members of the media scoured the Pacific Ballroom in search of the Hollywood elite and other VIPs attending the charity benefit for the Sickle Cell Disease Association.

Micah sat at a table surrounded by people from his artists and repertoire (A&R), publicity and product development departments.

They dined on a three-course meal: baby leaf lettuce

with marinated artichoke hearts and wedged Roma tomatoes and Dijon vinaigrette, breast of Mediterranean chicken served with sautéed artichokes, goat cheese mashed potatoes and herbed Italian vegetables, mascarpone caramel cake for dessert.

One of the groups from his label walked on stage to perform.

"Eden sounds great tonight," Sunni stated as she sliced off a piece of chicken and stuck it into his mouth.

Micah wiped his mouth with the edge of his napkin. "Yeah, she does," he agreed, silently wishing that he could've stayed home tonight.

He stood up and smiled politely when his generous donation was acknowledged along with a long thundering applause.

Sunni reached over and took his hand. "I still can't believe how shy you are when it comes to stuff like this. Honey, you are one of the good guys," she stated. "You should be walking around here with your head up high."

He gave her a narrowed glinting glance. "You know how I feel about being in the public eye, Sunni. I don't like being under a microscope."

"You're the CEO of a huge conglomerate, Micah," she responded, rising finely arched eyebrows. "You'd better get used to this because it's not going to go away."

Sunni took a sip of her hot tea.

Thirty minutes later, they left the ballroom. He had put in an appearance so as far as Micah was concerned, his work was done. He had a long day ahead of him and wanted to get some rest.

Micah escorted Sunni out of the hotel.

The driver brought their limo around, promptly stepped out and walked around to open the door.

"Micah, why don't we go back to your place?" she suggested with a seductive sparkle in her eye. "I'm not ready for the evening to end." She wound her arms inside his jacket and around his back.

Micah gave her a polite smile and resisted the urge to pull away. He knew Sunni wanted the media to photograph them in an embrace. She enjoyed being featured in gossip magazines and felt it enhanced her career.

"Sunni, it's late and I have a busy day tomorrow. I don't have any plans this weekend—maybe we can do something then."

"I'd love it. I haven't seen much of you lately."

He kissed her gently on the cheek. "We'll do something special then."

Sunni pulled him closer to her. "C'mere, I want a real kiss."

"I don't put on shows for the media," Micah stated. *"You know that."*

He ushered Sunni quickly into the car as paparazzi appeared out of nowhere, snapping pictures of them.

"How long have the two of you been dating, Micah?" someone shouted.

"Are you and Sunni thinking about marriage?" another yelled. "C'mon, give us the scoop."

Micah held up his hands in mock resignation. "I'm afraid there's nothing to tell. Have a good evening, everyone." He got into the car and the driver closed the door in haste.

"What *are* we doing?" Sunni asked when the car pulled away from the curb, merging with the traffic.

Micah did not want to have this conversation. He and Sunni had been spending time together for the past four or five months. She was stunning and he enjoyed her company, but Micah knew she had an agenda. She wanted a husband.

A rich husband.

It was not that he was opposed to marriage because he didn't want to marry. He wasn't in love with Sunni, which is why he hadn't taken their platonic relationship to the next level.

Sunni ran a French-manicured finger along his thigh. "Micah, you know how I feel about you. We are so good together. Why can't you see that? You need a woman like me as your wife."

He gave her an indulgent smile. "That's why we're such good friends."

"Micah, tell me, who did this to you?" Sunni asked.

Surprised by her question, he questioned, "Did what?"

"Hurt you," she responded. "Who broke your heart? That's the only reason I can think of that will explain why you keep this huge wall between us."

Micah did not respond.

"Well, whoever she is, she really did a number on you." Sunni ran a finger down his cheek. "I am a very patient woman, Micah. One day you'll see that I'm not here to cause you pain. If you give me the chance, I'd make you a very happy man."

He smiled. "I'm glad to have you in my life, Sunni. You are a very dear friend to me."

"There's that *friend* word again," she said with a mock sigh.

Micah laughed.

The limo slowed to a stop in front of her building.

"Will you give me a call tomorrow?" Sunni asked before stepping out of the car. "I know you talked about us getting together this weekend, but maybe we can meet for dinner. You still have to eat, you know?"

He nodded. "That's fine."

Micah stepped out of the car and walked Sunni to the door of her home. He kissed her cheek before saying good-night.

"It would've been," Sunni responded with a wink. "But it's your loss, honey. I would've rocked your world."

Micah chuckled. "I'm sure you would have."

She gave him a hug and then sauntered into the building, pausing briefly to speak to the man at the security desk.

Micah returned to the waiting limo.

Sunni was a nice girl and he enjoyed her companionship, but Micah had not fully opened his heart to another person since college. He didn't relish the thought of going home to an empty bed but cared too much to use Sunni in that way. Micah knew he would never give her what she was looking for.

One heartbreak was more than enough for him.

Tamara entered Sylvia's Restaurant looking for her Pi Beta Gamma soror, Kyra Dixon. She was running late for their lunch date due to a traffic accident on Washington Street S.W. near Memorial Drive.

Kyra was already seated at a table when Tamara entered the restaurant. She waved to get her attention.

"I'm so sorry I'm late," Tamara stated as she sat down in the chair across from her friend. "Have you ordered yet?"

"Not yet."

A waiter arrived minutes later prepared to take their orders.

"So how was your sister's wedding?" Kyra inquired after he left.

"Beautiful," Tamara responded with a smile. "My sister looked so happy and in love. It was very romantic."

"I guess the pressure's on for you to get married, huh?"

Tamara laughed. "Can you believe that my mother started in on me as soon as the service ended? We're standing there posing for pictures and she's asking me why I didn't bring a date to the wedding. She asked me if there was anyone serious in my life."

Kyra chuckled. "What did you tell her?"

"The truth," Tamara stated. "That I don't have a man and right now I'm not looking for one." She changed the subject and said, "Homecoming is a couple months away. Time moved by fast."

"Are you planning to attend the cocktail party on Friday?"

Tamara nodded. "I'll be there. Chloe wants me to cover the event for *Luster* magazine. I'm also thinking about doing a story on the fact that the alumni got together and agreed to donate money to restore the original administration building and use it as staff offices instead of tearing it down."

"Sounds good," Kyra said. "The school needs all the free press we can get."

The waiter returned, carrying a tray of food, which he set down on the table. Tamara blessed the food.

She sampled her gumbo while Kyra cut into her chicken.

"I'm actually looking forward to homecoming this year," Tamara announced. She didn't add that it was because Micah might be attending.

"It's going to be nice." Kyra stuck a forkful of macaroni into her mouth. "I can't wait. It's always good to see old friends."

Tamara agreed.

They continued making small talk as they finished off their meal.

"I need to get back to work," Tamara murmured, checking her watch when they were done eating.

"I can't believe how disciplined you are," Kyra declared. "If I worked at home, I think I'd be doing everything else around the house instead of focusing on my job."

An easy smile played at the corners of her mouth. "I like getting paid."

"As if you need the money," Kyra retorted with a chuckle. "Tamara, who are you trying to kid?"

"My mother has money," she corrected, pushing away from the table. "I don't."

After paying the check, she and Kyra rose up and walked out of the restaurant.

They paused at her car to hug.

"It was so good to see you," Tamara told her. "We should get together more often"

Kyra agreed. "We need to do this again real soon, soror."

"Sounds like a plan," Tamara responded. "Talk to you later."

Tamara got into her car and drove the two miles to her home in midtown.

The telephone rang as soon as she walked through the front door of her apartment.

"Hello," Tamara uttered.

"Hey, this is Samantha."

Tamara broke into a smile when she heard her editor's voice. They had recently discussed her becoming the features writer for the entertainment section.

"How would you like to interview Justice Kane?" Samantha asked. "You would have to fly out to Los Angeles for his album release party."

"I'd love it," she responded. Justice Kane was a performer signed to Micah's record company, Ross Red. If she did a great job on the story, this would better her chances in getting the position.

Tamara was sure that he would be attending the party so she considered this a sign. She would finally get that chance to mend her friendship with Micah. She knew that he never married and had read about his relationship with the model.

I had my chance and I blew it.

Micah hadn't only been her tutor but he'd been her friend—her best friend. They had spent a lot of time together. She and Micah used to attend the college football and basketball games together; there were times they went to the movies, clubs and even attended church together. Micah would even join Tamara on her visits to see her grandmother.

"This has to be a sign," she whispered.

Tamara knew that wanting to see Micah again had so much more to do with the fact that she was still in love with him. She had tried for years to get Micah out of her system, but to no avail—he still owned her heart.

She winced at the memory of how cruel she had been to Micah and desperately wanted the chance to explain why she had been so fearful of getting involved with him.

She prayed that once they sat down and talked he would understand and find it in his heart to forgive her.

Chapter 2

Tamara wanted to share her good news with someone, so she called Kyra later that evening. "Hey, girl… you won't believe where I'm going this weekend," she said when her friend answered the phone.

"Where?" Kyra questioned.

"Los Angeles," she announced. "I'm covering Justice Kane's album release party. *Luster* magazine wants me to do a story on him. Can you believe it?"

"That's great," Kyra responded with excitement. "Tamara, this is the kind of story you've been wanting to do for a long time. Hey, isn't Justice Kane with Micah's record company?"

"That's why I'm so excited," Tamara told Kyra. "I'm hoping to reconnect with him. I really miss our friendship."

"We used to have some good times back in the day. I used to try and get you to party with us, but you wanted to stay home and read. The only time we could get you out was when Micah asked you. Why didn't you two ever get together?" Kyra inquired. "I know you had feelings for him back then."

"Micah was my tutor and my friend," Tamara stated. "That's really all it was. I had too many issues for anything more."

"So you didn't have any feelings for him?"

"I didn't say that," Tamara answered. "Kyra, I was crazy about Micah, but the timing was all off and things just never worked out. You know how it goes."

"I always felt that something was bothering you," Kyra said. "It was just a feeling though because you were always walking around with a smile and you seemed really happy... still, I felt there was something."

Tamara considered Kyra one of her best friends, and they were close, spent time together often, but there were things from her past that she never shared with anyone—including her soror.

She had never told Kyra what happened between her and Micah on graduation night and decided against mentioning it now. Deep down, she didn't want anyone to know just how gullible she'd been back then.

"So what about now?"

"Kyra, he's seeing someone," Tamara responded. "His relationship with Sunni has been plastered all over the tabloids and *People* magazine." She tried to sound as neutral as possible.

"Tamara, you know that you can't believe everything you read in the tabloids. Micah says that he and that model are nothing but friends. At least that's what he told Kevin."

Kyra's words delighted Tamara. She silently prayed that her friend was right because the thought of Micah being involved in a serious relationship with another woman bothered her to the core.

"Whatever their relationship, I hope she doesn't trip if Micah and I grab a few minutes to sit down and talk when I get to Los Angeles," Tamara said.

"Tell him that I said hello when you see Micah," Kyra responded. "I'm so proud of that boy. He came from the Greenwood projects, and look at him now. He left us back here in Atlanta and really made a success of his life. Now all he needs is the right woman to share it with."

Tamara had to hide her inner feelings as a sense of inadequacy swept over her. She thought about Kyra's words and wondered if after all this time had passed if she had anything to offer Micah.

Like everyone else, Tamara had her own share of past pain and trauma but she had worked past the betrayal of trust, discovered her wholeness, the experience shaping her in a way that no other has.

She learned early on that along with happiness, life brought pain. Her grandmother had taught Tamara that in order to heal, she had to forgive and that forgiveness is essential as a means of personal transformation.

Tamara still had seeds of unforgiveness rooted in her. She desired forgiveness, but until she could forgive she would never be completely free.

She and Kyra stayed on the phone for almost an hour, talking about their college days and the upcoming Pi Beta Gamma fundraiser.

After promising to get together soon, Tamara ended the call, then stood up and walked over to the window to stare out at the beautiful Atlanta skyline.

"I miss you so much, Micah," she whispered.

Amused, Micah hung up the telephone, but not before Samantha, the editor of *Luster* magazine, thanked him for the fifth or sixth time during their conversation.

He took a deep breath and tried to relax now that the initial part of his plan had succeeded.

He and Tamara would finally come face-to-face again after ten years. Micah wasn't sure how he would feel about seeing her again, so he decided that this meeting would have to happen in a place he could control. It would give him the upper hand.

Micah called and arranged to have Tamara attend the party at the Vanguard Club in Beverly Hills. However, she would have to deal with him first before he allowed her access to Justice Kane.

He wanted a glimpse of the woman Tamara had become, but he also wanted to settle an old score.

His heart bore a permanent scar seared by her rejection. The fact that Micah still harbored deep feelings for Tamara only fueled his anger more. He struggled with loving her and knowing that she thought he wasn't good enough for her.

A few days ago, he typed in her name while online out of curiosity and found a photo of her on *Luster* magazine's Web site. That's when he came up with the idea for the interview and a way to get back at her.

Tamara looked much younger than her thirty-two

years and from the looks of it, wore her shoulder-length hair natural and without chemicals, the warm brown color complimenting her light chocolate complexion and hazel-green eyes.

She's still beautiful, he thought to himself.

Micah forced himself to remember the way she had treated him. A computer science major in college, he was the quiet, shy geek who tutored Tamara in math during her freshman year—their friendship birthed out of the tutoring sessions.

He had always thought Tamara was sweet, caring and felt extremely comfortable around her. Micah had even believed that she thought of him as more than a tutor. During their time in college, Micah never once saw signs of Tamara being a snob or elitist—she had always been down-to-earth.

His mouth tightened as he thought about graduation night—the night that Micah made the mistake of confessing his feelings for her. He had even planned to propose marriage; however, he never got that far.

Tamara rejected Micah, telling him directly that she would never date anyone like him. She didn't need him to tutor her anymore. She had landed a job with the *Atlanta Daily Journal* so she had no more use for him.

It was then that Micah realized he did not know her as well as he had initially thought. He never knew she held even the tiniest interest in writing. Micah knew that she kept a journal, but to him that did not necessarily mean she wanted to be a writer.

It had come as a complete surprise when Tamara announced she was going to work as an entry-level journalist with the newspaper. Her degree was in business and not journalism.

If they had been as close as Micah thought they were, why would she keep her love for writing a secret? What else had she been keeping from him?

Micah Ross was *fine*.

Tamara laid a back issue of *Ebony* with Micah gracing the cover down on the chair beside her.

She kept that issue on her coffee table since its release two years ago.

Micah pretty much looked as he did back in college except that he no longer wore those black-framed glasses that Tamara used to think were so sexy on him.

His skin was the color of dark chocolate, smooth and free of facial hair. Those dark brown eyes of his were so intense that she believed they could pierce through stone.

Her heart raced at the prospect of seeing him again.

"I've got to talk to you," she whispered to his likeness on the magazine. "Micah, I feel bad about the things I said to you on graduation night. I really hope you'll give me a chance to apologize and explain why I reacted that way."

I never should have listened to those other boys. I realize that now.

The telephone rang.

Tamara checked the caller ID before answering. "Hello, Mama."

"Sweetie, are you busy right now?"

"No, what's up?"

"I'm here at Lexington's Restaurant. Since it's right down the street from your neighborhood, why don't you come have dinner with me?"

"Give me ten minutes," Tamara told her. "I'll be there."

"See you then," Jillian stated.

Tamara went into her bathroom to freshen up. She looked down at her jeans and decided on impulse to change clothes. Her mother would be dressed up—Jillian was always dressed in designer suits and expensive shoes.

I've never seen my mother in a pair of jeans or a sweat suit, she thought with amusement. Dressing down for Jillian meant a pair of khakis or linen pants.

Tamara changed into a black linen sundress, silver sandals and accessories. She knew that her mother would approve, as the dress was a gift from her.

She arrived at the restaurant fifteen minutes later.

Her mother was already seated. Tamara almost turned around and left when she realized that her mother was not alone.

I should have known she was up to something.

Jillian didn't care much for Lexington's but came here because she knew that Tamara was less likely to refuse her since it was only a couple blocks away from her apartment.

"Hello, Mama." The greeting was forced at best.

Tamara was furious with her mother for hijacking her into a blind date.

"Dear, I want you to meet Anthony. His mother and I went to high school together. He just moved to Atlanta, and I thought you two should meet. Anthony, this is my daughter Tamara."

She plastered on a smile. "It's nice to meet you, Anthony."

Tamara sent her mother a sharp look as she took a seat.

"So, Anthony, what brings you to Atlanta?" she asked.

"I'll be working at Fitzgerald & Johnson Industries as lead counsel," he said. "Your mother tells me that you write for *Luster* magazine."

"I do," she confirmed.

Tamara was struggling to keep her temper in check. Why couldn't Jillian just mind her own business? She didn't need her mother's help in getting a man.

She managed to enjoy herself while they ate. Anthony had a wonderful sense of humor, and he could hold an intelligent conversation on several subjects. He was definitely an improvement over the last one her mother had tried to set Tamara up with.

Anthony asked for her number.

Feeling pressured, Tamara gave it to him. If she hadn't, her mother would have given it to him anyway.

Jillian excused herself to go to the ladies' room.

She was about to follow her, but Anthony stopped her.

"Tamara, look, it's no pressure. Let's just get through this dinner to appease our mothers."

She gave him the first genuine smile of the evening. "You have one of those interfering mothers, too?"

Anthony nodded. "I'm in a relationship, but she doesn't think Rochelle is the woman for me. I know what I want and that is Rochelle. However, I hope that the three of us can get together sometime. Maybe we can all become friends."

"I'd like that, Anthony."

He paid the bill, then told Jillian that he had to leave.

"Tamara, I know that you're upset," she said when Anthony walked out of the restaurant. "But I saw the way you two were interacting." She broke into a smile. "Admit it. Don't you like him just a little bit?"

"Yeah, I do," Tamara responded. "Actually I like him a lot. In fact, I think he's the man for me, Mama." She gazed into her mother's hazel-green eyes and said, "Anthony has a girlfriend. We're going to have a threesome when I get back from Los Angeles."

"WHAT?"

She burst into laughter at the look of horror on her mother's face.

Jillian gasped and couldn't seem to catch her breath. Tamara reached over and took her hand. "Mama, I'm kidding."

Her mother patted her face with the napkin. "I can't believe you'd say something like that."

"It's what you deserved," Tamara countered. "Mama, please stop trying to set me up on blind dates. Don't you think I'm capable of finding my own man?"

Jillian's lips puckered in silence.

Tamara chuckled. "Good point. I haven't done a great job in that department, either."

"I just want to see you happily married with a family."

"Then let it happen naturally, Mama."

Jillian gave a stiff nod. "Now what is this about you going to Los Angeles?"

She told her mother about the assignment and seeing Micah again.

"It sounds promising," Jillian stated. "I can't wait to hear all about the trip."

Tamara pushed away from the table and rose to her feet. "There you go again. Mama, I'll see you later."

Jillian followed her out of the restaurant.

"Mama, why don't you look for a man for you?" Tamara suggested. "You should try to find someone to spend the rest of your life with instead of trying to shape my future."

A shadow of sadness colored Jillian's expression. "I don't think I can ever trust another man. Not after…" Her voice died.

Tamara hugged her mother. "I had a great time tonight but you are forbidden to arrange any more blind dates. You're making me feel insecure."

Jillian placed a hand to her face. "Oh, nooo…"

"I'm kidding, Mama," Tamara uttered with a laugh. "I need to get home and pack."

"I love you."

"I love you, too, Mama."

Before she headed home, Tamara waited for Jillian to get into her car and leave the restaurant parking lot.

Tamara rehearsed exactly what she would say repeatedly in her head for the rest of the evening and again the next morning as she prepared to leave for the airport.

Tamara flew first class from Atlanta to Los Angeles, both anxious and excited about seeing Micah again.

She hoped that he would be the one picking her up at the airport so that he could clear the air before meeting his performer. It would help the interview along if there was no tension between them.

Maybe I'm making too much of this. Micah's not the type of man who would hold a grudge.

To quell her nervousness, Tamara documented her thoughts.

August 28th

At this very moment, I am on a plane en route to Los Angeles to interview one of Micah's performers. I have mixed feelings about this little reunion because of what happened before we graduated college. Hopefully, Micah will put the past behind us and give me a chance to explain.

I have never forgotten that look of absolute hurt in his eyes. I have never been filled with such guilt as I experienced then. I'm not really sure an apology is enough to undo the hurt.

What if I've overanalyzed that moment? What if what I thought was hurt was actually something else?

I guess this is why Micah and I need to have a conversation. I miss him and deeply wish to repair our friendship.

I just hope that it isn't too late to make amends.

Most girls had considered Micah a nerd back in the day—but not Tamara.

Sexy Chocolate.

That's what she used to call Micah behind his back. He stood six-three, and even with glasses, the man looked good.

She remembered how the basketball coach wanted Micah to play for the school but he refused. Instead, he preferred to focus on his academics and his dedication paid off.

Micah utilized his talent and dual degrees in business and computer science to build his empire, Ross Red.

She was proud of him and his accomplishments and hoped for the chance to tell him so.

Things ended so abruptly that night. Tamara didn't know if they could ever truly mend the rift in their relationship, but she was willing to try. Micah's friendship meant the world to her.

She settled back against her seat and closed her eyes. A thread of apprehension snaked through her body when the pilot announced they would be landing in twenty minutes.

I can do this.

Tamara repeated this over and over in her mind, trying to convince herself. Not that it was working. She was extremely nervous at the thought of seeing Micah again.

She assumed that he would be the one meeting her plane, and once they got over the awkward moments, they could talk and Tamara could tell him everything.

Thirty-five minutes later, she stepped off the plane and made her way through the Los Angeles International Airport. Tamara was disappointed when she didn't see Micah at the gate.

Maybe he was waiting for her in the baggage-claim area.

Instead, she found a man in a dark suit holding up a sign with her name on it. She walked up to him and identified herself. "Hi, I'm Tamara Hodges."

"I hope you had a comfortable flight," he said. "If you give me your ticket, I'll retrieve your luggage for you, Ms. Hodges."

"Thanks," she murmured. "It's red. There are two bags. One large and a medium."

Tamara stood near the exit doors as she waited for her driver to bring her luggage.

He navigated to Tamara and led her outside to the car.

According to her itinerary, she was booked at the Four Seasons Hotel Los Angeles. While en route, Tamara checked her voice mail and returned two missed phone calls. She had hoped to find a message from Micah but it was to no avail.

He was a busy man—she knew that, but Tamara really thought that since he had given the interview his blessing he was ready to reconnect with her.

Now she wasn't so sure.

Micah positioned himself in the lobby area of the hotel where a suite had been reserved for Tamara. He wanted to catch a glimpse of the woman who had broken his heart.

He checked his watch.

She should be arriving at any moment.

He sensed her presence before she actually walked through the doors and up to the lobby.

Tamara was still slender with curves in all the right places, Micah noted as he watched her check into the hotel.

He raised his newspaper to shield his face when she turned to glance around the lobby.

The way she kept looking around, Micah wondered if she was looking for him.

Probably, but it didn't matter.

Micah determined that Tamara would not see him until he was ready for a face-to-face with her. The way his heart was racing and his eyes caressing her body—

it was still too soon. He needed more time to rein in his emotions.

From outward appearances, Tamara looked fragile but Micah knew that she possessed a quiet strength—a quality that had drawn him to her all those years ago.

He watched as Tamara strolled over to the elevators and waited. Her eyes traveled the luxury surroundings once more before stepping inside.

Micah waited until the doors closed before rising to his feet and taking his leave.

His cell phone rang.

It was his secretary, Bette, informing him that his guest had arrived safely and was at the hotel. She also reminded him of his meeting with the art director that was scheduled in an hour.

"Thank you, Bette. I'm on my way back to the office now." Micah got up, strode through the glass revolving doors and handed the valet his ticket.

The love of his life was here in Los Angeles, and he was still avoiding her. He had a wall erected around his heart, but Tamara—was a trigger for him, which is why Micah purposed not to see her until he was in control of his emotions.

Micah stood outside, waiting for his car to arrive. The valet attendant pulled the car in front of him and got out. Micah tipped him and strode around to the driver side.

He experienced a strange sensation, which caused the hair on the back of his neck to stand up.

Micah turned around.

Tamara was standing inside the lobby, looking at him through the glass wall, her expression one of complete shock.

His emotions unsettled, Micah pretended he did not recognize her, stepped into his car and quickly drove away. It had been a mistake coming here, he decided.

Micah knew that he and Tamara would come face-to-face, and when they did it would be on his terms. Micah vowed to make her pay for the pain she caused him all those years ago.

He had done nothing but try to be a good friend to Tamara, but the way she turned on him graduation night proved that their relationship had been one-sided in reality. Micah tried to forget about her over the years, but his heart would not let him.

As much as I want to hate Tamara, I can't. I am still in love with a woman who believes I'll never be good enough for her.

In his college days, Micah had been more of a geek and was not the kind of boy most girls usually went for, but his job as a tutor placed him in a circle of people he wouldn't otherwise hang with. Out of those relationships, friendships formed.

He thought Tamara was different from any other girl he had ever known. She was on the quiet side, kept to herself most of the time when she wasn't with her sorority sisters. On the weekends, she liked visiting her grandmother—he would go with her from time to time.

Micah had been there to comfort Tamara when the woman died. He didn't remember exactly the moment he fell in love with her, but when he landed the job with a software company in Chicago and was due to leave the week following graduation, Micah didn't want to leave Tamara without letting her know how he felt.

That was indubitably the biggest mistake of his life

because she crushed him with her rejection. Tamara had tried to contact him a few days later, but Micah was hurt and preparing to relocate to Chicago.

Chapter 3

Tamara rushed out of the hotel but failed to get there in time to catch Micah.

She thought for a moment that he had seen her, too. Apparently, he hadn't or didn't recognize her. Tamara had come back downstairs to visit the gift shop but seeing Micah distracted her from her purpose.

Disappointed, Tamara returned to her suite, settled down on the sofa and pulled out her cell phone.

She sat in the chair for a moment, her thin fingers tensed in her lap to calm her nerves. Tamara inhaled and exhaled slowly, opened her phone and dialed. "Hello, this is Tamara Hodges. Do you have a contact number for Micah Ross please? I'm here to do a story on Justice Kane, and I really need to speak with him."

"I'm sorry but Mr. Ross is out of the office."

Tamara doubted they would give out his mobile number so she didn't bother asking for it. Instead, she inquired, "Would you take down my number and ask him to call me please?"

"What is the number?"

She gave the secretary her cell-phone number and the one to the hotel.

"I'll give him the message as soon as he returns, Ms. Hodges."

"Thank you." Tamara stirred uneasily in the chair, her uncertainty increasing by the minute. She didn't want to consider that Micah still held a grudge where she was concerned or that he didn't want to talk to her.

Tamara strolled out onto one of the two balconies to enjoy the panoramic views of the Hollywood Hills and downtown Los Angeles. She stayed out there for the next fifteen minutes just basking in the late summer sun. It was a clear day with no smog in sight.

She navigated back into the sitting area, which was furnished with two armchairs and a sofa set around a glass-top coffee table, a writing desk, plasma TV and entertainment system.

The bedroom, decorated in a soothing neutral color with muted gold accents, offered a high-back armchair and side table, a second plasma television and large walk-in closet with dark wood furnishings and a comfortable looking king-size bed.

While she waited for Micah's call, Tamara unpacked her suitcase and her laptop to keep busy.

When Tamara put away all of her clothes, she sat down at the desk and opened up the computer to work on an article she needed to finish before the week was out.

Tamara stole a peek at the clock.

Thirty minutes had passed.

She considered making another call to Micah but silently reasoned her way out of calling. The man was busy, and she didn't want to become a pest. Tamara could not escape the feeling that maybe he was avoiding her.

"Please call me, Micah," she whispered in the empty room. "I really want to talk to you."

Tamara had hoped they could have dinner together later this evening, so she made another call to his office.

She received the same response as before.

Tamara replaced the receiver in the cradle. "Micah..." she whispered.

Two hours passed and still no word from Micah. Tamara ordered room service because she didn't feel like eating alone in the hotel restaurant.

Micah was apparently too busy to speak with her; he was working or maybe he had a date with Sunni. Hope sprang up in Tamara as she considered that she and Micah would both be attending the release party, so at some point they would have to talk.

Samantha called her shortly after eight.

"I just spoke with Micah Ross, and we came up with another idea," she stated. "What do you think about the idea of going on tour with Justice Kane? At least for the West Coast cities anyway. You'll be traveling with the artist on the tour bus and writing about the behind-the-scenes action you observe firsthand for our readers. Write the story as if the readers are there with you."

"This sounds like a great idea," Tamara said. "Samantha, I'm all for it. I'm glad I overpacked for this trip."

"Great. You'll e-mail the series of articles as you finish them."

"You said Micah Ross is fine with this?" she asked. Tamara was surprised, considering that she hadn't been able to catch up to him. Why didn't he call her directly? She wondered.

"It was actually his idea," Samantha responded. "This article will let us know if you're ready to become a feature writer for the magazine. This is your shot, Tamara."

"I realize that. I won't let you down, Samantha."

"I know that. Enjoy yourself, Tamara, and e-mail those articles as soon as you finish them."

Tamara broke into a smile. Even though she hadn't heard a word from Micah, it seemed as if he were trying to keep her around for a little longer; however, she wished that he had called her directly to discuss his thoughts.

Another thought struck her. Maybe he was deliberately avoiding her.

"I called Micah's office earlier but haven't been able to speak to him directly," Tamara stated. "I'm assuming we'll touch base sometime tomorrow."

"Oh, he did tell me that he's going to be in meetings all day tomorrow but said that he'll see you at the release party."

Tamara hid her disappointment. Micah's schedule was so tight that she wondered if she would have the chance to apologize. The party just was not the place to bring up the past.

She and her editor discussed one of her other projects before ending their conversation.

A commercial flashed across the television. A thread

of jealousy snaked down her spine as she watched a smiling Sunni saunter across the screen wearing the newest bra from Victoria's Secret.

What does Micah see in her? Tamara wondered. She's tall, thin and beautiful, but is she truly in love with him? How does Micah feel about her? Did he love her, too?

She couldn't tell from the many photographs she had seen of the two of them.

Micah rarely made eye contact with the media. They considered him aloof and even a bit eccentric.

Tamara knew that Micah wasn't aloof—just shy and had always been uncomfortable in the spotlight. She wondered if any of the reporters knew that he could sing and that he played the piano, drums and sax. He also loved computers and could write software programs. Even though he studied business and computer science in school, Micah's first love had always been music.

She was pretty sure that those same reporters also didn't know how much he loved reading, his tastes varying from Shakespeare to James Patterson. Micah rarely granted personal interviews, instead focusing on his A-list of performers and pushing their careers forward. He was an astute executive and knew the music industry inside and out.

While the media and other industry professionals considered him a man of mystery, they held him in high regard.

"How could I have been so stupid and so insensitive?" she whispered. "How could I ever have thought he was like…" Tamara shook her head and rose to her feet.

She opened the floor-to-ceiling curtains and stared

out the window over the city of Los Angeles. It was so beautiful at night. Tamara loved California and often came to visit her family living in Oceanside, a coastal town near San Diego.

She could not fully enjoy the night air, the shining stars and the moon because Micah dominated her thoughts.

Tamara spent the rest of her evening editing and revising her article about a woman who had overcome breast cancer and was now inspiring others.

An hour passed and still no word from Micah.

Then another.

When the clock struck eleven, Tamara gave up and decided to go to bed. She was still on East Coast time and feeling weary.

Tamara vowed she would not leave Los Angeles until she and Micah had a chance to sit down and talk.

Micah eyed the telephone, still warring within himself whether or not to call Tamara.

She was probably in bed by now he thought and mentally let himself off the hook.

Old feelings that he thought were long buried had resurfaced after seeing her today, and he had not been able to get her off his mind.

Along with those feelings came another emotion— resentment. He hungered to make Tamara pay for the way she used him back then. Micah believed that the only reason Tamara was reaching out to him now was the interview he had arranged.

He wondered what would happen if she didn't deliver the interview as promised and if it would hurt her career.

Micah's lips curled upward at the thought.

Tamara needed this interview to take place if she ever wanted to be considered for something other than writing fluff on debutante balls, charity events and flower shows.

His stomach growled, reminding him that he had missed lunch. It was after eight and he didn't like to eat heavy when it was late so he made himself a salad and heated up a piece of leftover grilled salmon.

Sunni called Micah, wanting to know if she could come over to spend the evening with him. She had been trying to seduce him for months now. He wasn't about to let her into his bed because Micah didn't have any idea what it would eventually cost him to get her out.

"Not tonight. Sunni, I've got a lot of work to catch up on," Micah told her. "I need to stay focused."

"Micah, you've been a real party pooper lately. You used to have time for me."

"Sunni, I have a business to run. You know that."

"You have very capable people working for you, too," she retorted.

"I'll give you a call later," he stated.

Micah knew that she was not happy with his response, but the truth was that he really did not feel like having company tonight. He wanted to spend the rest of his evening deciding exactly what to do about Tamara Hodges.

Tamara called and left another message for Micah after she ate her breakfast. His secretary told her that he was in a meeting and would not be returning calls until later in the day. She did not expect any other response.

She was sure that Micah was avoiding her. If he were not, Tamara was positive that she would have heard from him by now. This was not her first trip to Los Angeles, so Tamara decided against leaving the hotel for sightseeing or shopping. Instead, she spent her day in the hotel room working on another project until it was time to dress for the party.

Tamara's nerves had been on edge all day long. She even took an instant dislike to everything she packed for the trip and now wished she had gone shopping earlier.

After her shower, Tamara changed into a black Tadashi dress with a sheer top, sleeves and shutter pleating from bodice to the hem.

"This is so not me," she mumbled as she stared at her reflection in the floor-length mirror. The dress hugged her body lovingly, but Tamara wasn't comfortable when it came to showing off her curves.

Next, she slipped on a Proenza Schouler georgette dress that she'd snagged on sale for two hundred seventy-two dollars at Sak's Fifth Avenue department store the day before she left Atlanta.

The black-and-white print, dramatically gathered shift draped at the back with a floating train. The dress looked great with the opaque black stockings and Christian Louboutin open-toe patent-leather pumps.

"Not bad," she whispered. "But I just don't think it's right for this event." Tamara decided she would save this dress for the Hollington College homecoming weekend. She would wear it to the reception.

So what am I wearing tonight?

The new pumps were already torturing her feet, so Tamara practically kicked them off.

"I'm working tonight so I need to be comfortable," Tamara said as she pulled out another dress. She changed again, this time into a Vera Wang silk halter dress in a vivid emerald-green color.

Tamara put on a pair of silver and emerald jeweled thong sandals with straps that wrapped around her ankles. She added an emerald ring, white gold and emerald bangles with matching earrings to complete her look.

She undid her twists and fingered through her hair, combing through the waves. Tamara applied her make-up with a light hand and surveyed the results. Satisfied, she walked out of the bathroom.

How will Micah respond when he sees me again? She wondered. Will he be happy to see me?

Tamara was looking forward to seeing him again after all these years but didn't know how she would handle seeing him with another woman.

Micah, his secretary, the event planner and the owner of the club walked from room to room, making sure that everything was exactly the way it should be. He was very hands-on and always liked to do a final walk-through before any of his events.

"Where will our sponsors be seated?" Micah asked the event coordinator.

"Over here," she responded, pointing to the right of where they were standing on the stage. "Just as you requested."

He awarded her a smile. "Thank you."

She glanced down at her watch and excused herself to make sure all the staff was in place for the event.

Micah felt that familiar sensation. He felt Tamara's presence before he actually saw her.

He turned around to find her walking toward him.

Their eyes met, and Tamara broke into a beautiful smile. "Micah, it's so good to see you. It's been a long time," she murmured.

"Ten years," he responded. Micah couldn't believe that she was standing in front of him acting as if she had not ripped his heart out.

"Can you believe it?" Tamara asked as if trying to lull him into a conversation. "We've been out of school for *ten* years."

Although she was trying to hide it, Micah could tell that Tamara was very nervous. He heard it in her voice. She wanted to be all warm and fuzzy, but it was not gonna happen. Micah knew that it was only because she wanted this story on Justice Kane.

His heart thudded once and then settled back to its natural rhythm. She was even more gorgeous than Micah remembered.

"Tamara, you haven't changed at all," Micah stated. It was not meant to be a compliment.

"You're so sweet for saying that, but I do own a couple of mirrors and they don't lie."

Their eyes locked as their breathing seemed to come in unison.

A tall leggy woman wearing a curve hugging, one-shoulder beaded mini dress with stellar results approached them, breaking the tiny thread that drew them like a drug.

Ignoring Tamara completely, she slipped an arm around Micah and said, "I've been looking for you, darling. Are you ready to sit down?"

Tamara was not about to just disappear into the woodwork. She held out her hand and introduced herself, saying, "Hi, I'm Tamara Hodges. I'm here to do a story on Justice Kane."

The woman eyed her from head to toe, a smirk on her flawless face. "I'm sure you know that I'm Sunni. It's nice to meet you."

Tamara didn't acknowledge one way or another. Instead, she glanced over at Micah as if waiting for him to say something, but it was Sunni who broke the silence.

"What magazine do you write for?" she asked.

"*Luster*," Tamara responded.

"I was featured on their cover a couple months ago." Sunni ran her fingers through her long spiral curls. "They couldn't keep that issue in print."

Tamara pasted on a polite smile. "I remember."

There was no point in telling the deluded woman that the issue did not sell out because of her face on the cover—it was because it was a special fashion issue.

Slipping her arm through Micah's, Sunni said, "Make sure you get lots of photos of me and Micah."

Tamara glanced over at him, noting the amused glint in his eyes. He was enjoying this while Sunni was getting on her last nerve. Tamara took great delight in reminding her, "The story is on Justice, his life and music."

Her cell phone rang.

"If you two will excuse me…I need to take this call." Tamara walked away, leaving him alone with Sunni.

She stole a peek over her shoulder. Micah was gazing

down lovingly at Sunni. Even from where she was standing, Tamara could see that he cared deeply for her.

She felt the edges of jealousy pulling at her. Kyra didn't know what she was talking about—Micah and Sunni were definitely involved from the way they were acting.

Tamara, get yourself together, she silently chided herself. *Why are you acting like this? You have no right to be jealous or possessive.*

She stole another look over her shoulder and found Micah standing there watching her. There was something in his expression that indicated he wasn't all that happy to see her again.

Tamara was even more determined to talk to Micah so that she could straighten things out between them. She was going to have to pry him out of Sunni's viselike grip. The woman wanted to make sure that she knew they were a couple. Tamara did note that while he was very attentive to Sunni, he had never been a man who openly displayed affection but she could sense an intimacy between them.

She was so caught up in her musings that she did not notice that they had walked up behind her.

"Tamara," he prompted, touching her arm lightly.

"Huh?" Embarrassed, she glanced up to find him and Sunni watching her.

"I'm sorry, were you saying something to me?"

His brown eyes met her hazel-green ones, probing to her very soul. "Tamara, I asked if you wanted something to drink."

"A glass of white wine please."

Micah signaled a waiter and placed their orders.

They stood for a moment in uncomfortable silence

until Sunni stated, "I see someone I need to speak to, honey, but I won't be long. Please excuse me."

"I'm glad we have a few minutes alone," Tamara began as she tried to force her confused emotions into order. "I would like to sit down with you and talk, Micah. There's a lot I have to tell you."

"So talk," he responded, his expression a mask of stone.

Taken aback by the coolness of his tone, Tamara quickly noted that Micah was no longer the same man she knew all those years ago. He had changed.

"Micah, this is supposed to be a party," she reminded him with a nervous chuckle. "I don't want to do this here, but I do want to talk about this another time— maybe tomorrow if you're not busy."

He did not respond immediately.

Their drinks arrived.

He handed her the glass of wine.

"Thank you," she said and took a sip. "Mmm... this is good."

Again Tamara's words were met with silence.

She released a short sigh of frustration. "Micah, will you please talk to me?"

"Tamara, what are we supposed to be talking about? You really haven't said anything."

She took a deep breath and adjusted her smile. It was clear that Micah wasn't going to make this easy for her. "Okay... Well, let's talk about Justice. First off, I really want to thank you for allowing me to go on tour with him. This opportunity is going to guarantee my position as the feature writer for the entertainment section of *Luster* magazine and take my career to the next level for sure. This is my trial run so I really can't mess this up. Micah, I've got some great ideas about this story and I—"

"Actually, I'm glad you brought that up," Micah stated. "I've changed my mind. After further consideration, I've decided that the interview may not be a good idea for my artist. As you know, Justice Kane has come a long way from being that thug from the ATL, and I'm just not sure it makes good business sense to bring his past back up. You *were* planning to write from the hometown bad boy gone good angle, weren't you?"

Tamara finished her glass of wine in one swallow. "You can't be serious about killing the article, Micah. Justice *has* come a long way from the person he used to be—why not write about his journey to the man he is now? His story would inspire others, don't you think?"

His hard gaze met hers. "I've never been more serious in my life."

Chapter 4

I've never been more serious in my life.

She had said those very same words to him ten years ago. In fact, they were the last words she had spoken to him on graduation night. Right after she told Micah that she would never date someone like him.

Tamara still remembered the hurt expression on his face. When he asked her if she was serious, she had replied that she'd never been more serious in her life.

Granted, she had treated him badly a long time ago, but now he was messing with her career.

A wave of hot fury washed over Tamara. "Micah, I don't know what's going on with you. I came to Los Angeles under the impression that you were fine with me interviewing Justice."

His expression was a mask of stone. "As I've said, I changed my mind."

Tamara held her temper in check when Micah's secretary joined them briefly to let him know that Justice Kane had arrived.

"Would you mind telling me why?" she demanded when Bette left to complete the next item on her to-do list. "Micah, why are you acting this way?"

Micah frowned as if he were irritated by her question. "After further consideration, I just don't think this is the right direction we should go in right now. If you will excuse me, I need to check on some things backstage," he told her, his tone cold and exact. "Enjoy your evening, Ms. Hodges."

He stood up and walked off without waiting for her response.

Tamara chewed on her bottom lip and tried to control her anger. She knew that she had treated Micah badly in college but the man she knew and loved would never set out to destroy her career just to prove a point.

Or would he?

One thing was for sure, she did not intend to just give up.

Tamara caught the eye of Bette, the secretary, and got up to speak with her. "Is there any way I can go backstage? I'd like to get some comments from Justice."

"That's fine, Ms. Hodges," she responded. "Your press pass will allow you entry."

Tamara walked through the double doors with purpose. Micah was in the hallway talking to one of the band members.

He stepped into her path, showing no signs of relenting. "Tamara, what are you doing back here? I thought I'd made myself clear that there will be no interview."

"Micah, I get it," Tamara said, cutting him off. She kept all expression from her voice as she talked. "Okay…I get it. I hurt you. Look, I didn't want to do this here, which is why I have been calling you and even tonight—I tried getting you to commit to a time when we could talk."

Keeping her voice low, she continued. "Micah, I'm sorry for the way that I treated you in college. I really am, but when I heard those boys talking about how you were planning to sleep with me graduation night—I was so hurt."

Tamara paused a moment before adding, "Back then, I was going through a lot of stuff, and I couldn't believe that you had been planning something like that."

"I never said anything like that. I would think that you would've known me better than that, but I guess you don't."

"Deep down I knew that you weren't that type of person, but I'd already said some pretty cruel things to you. I didn't know how to come back to you and apologize. I could never take back the words."

"We were all going through something, Tamara. I just wish you had come to me and asked if I'd said whatever you heard instead of believing the rumor."

"I realize that now, Micah. What you don't understand is that something happened to me that had me really messed up for a long time." Tamara took a deep breath and then exhaled slowly. "You know, I actually thought that I would come out here and apologize and that you'd forgive me. I thought that we'd be able to move past the hurt and be professional, Micah."

Her angry gaze met his. "Tell me something. Did you

set all of this in motion to deliberately hurt me?" she asked. "Are you that thirsty for revenge? The difference between you and me is that I never set out to hurt you deliberately. I made a mistake, Micah. But none of that matters, huh?"

Without waiting for a response, Tamara turned and walked away.

She asked the valet to alert her driver that she was ready to leave. While she waited, Tamara struggled to keep her tears at bay.

When her car arrived, she got in and returned to the hotel.

Tamara waited until she was in her hotel suite before breaking down in tears. She had not been prepared to face Micah's wrath. She never considered that those seeds of rejection she planted in him had sprouted into a wall of bitterness.

He actually hates me enough to try and ruin my career.

The thought saddened Tamara as ten long years of regret assailed her. He was no longer the man she knew in college. That much was obvious.

Grief and despair tore at her heart over the loss of a man who was once a very dear friend.

How could she have been so stupid?

She should have realized all along that Micah was still upset with her. It probably would have been a good idea to insist on talking to him before making the trip.

Tamara sighed, then gave a resigned shrug.

She considered calling Samantha, but it was three hours later on the East Coast—well past midnight in Atlanta. Besides, she had no idea how to explain what happened. Tamara ignored the heavy feeling in her stomach and began to pack.

"What happened to that reporter girl?" Sunni asked when she walked backstage to join Micah.

"She's not a reporter girl, Sunni," Micah stated. "But to answer your question, Tamara's probably out front at our table."

Sunni shook her head. "No, she's not. I just left there." She played with her curly tendrils. "Matter of fact, I haven't seen her in a while. I thought that maybe Tamara had come back here to talk to Justice or hang up under you."

His eyes searching around the room, Micah pulled out his cell phone and called his secretary. "Bette, have you seen Tamara?"

"She left about twenty minutes ago, Mr. Ross. Would you like me to contact Ms. Hodges for you?"

"No," Micah stated. "I'll take care of this myself."

"What are you going to do?" Sunni asked after he ended the call.

"I need to leave for a little while, but I'll be back before Justice performs."

A thread of guilt ran down his spine over the way Micah had treated Tamara. It was childish, and he now regretted his actions.

Sunni glared at him. "I can't believe you're going to run out on me like this. You're going after her, aren't you? Micah, is there something going on that I should know about?"

"Look, Sunni, she was an old friend of mine from college and I haven't seen her in almost ten years. We had a misunderstanding," Micah explained. "I need to apologize to her."

It was clear that Sunni was not happy about this sudden turn of events. "I'm sure it can wait until after the party. There is no way that I'm letting you abandon me—the media will be all over something like this. Besides, I doubt Tamara will be going anywhere tonight. She wants you to come running after her."

"Sunni, this is not your call. I won't be gone long."

"Whatever," she muttered; her eyes were stony with anger.

Micah had his driver take him to the Four Seasons Hotel Los Angeles. The car had barely stopped before he was out and rushing into the lobby. He took the elevator up to the sixteenth floor suite and knocked on the door.

Tamara opened the door as if she had been expecting him, but the expression on her face told him otherwise.

"I thought you were room service," she said. "Micah, what are you doing here? I figured after the way you were treating me earlier that you didn't want to be around me. If you came to kick me out, then you don't have to bother. I'm flying home on the first flight to the ATL."

"I'm here because it's my turn to apologize to you. May I please come inside?"

Surprised, Tamara stepped aside to let Micah enter the room and then closed the door. "You should be at the release party. There's no need to worry about me. I'm a big girl." She stood with her hands on her hips, waiting.

"I'm sorry, Tamara. I don't want to ruin your career—that was never really my intent."

"What was your intent then?" Tamara asked, folding her arms across her chest.

A loud knock on the door placed a temporary break in their conversation.

Micah glanced over at her. "Are you expecting someone?" He hoped that Sunni hadn't decided to up and follow him to the hotel.

"It should be my food," she announced. "I ordered room service."

Micah took care of the bill despite her objections.

After the server left, Tamara sat down at a table and removed the lid covering her meal. "Have some," she offered. "I remember how much you used to love French fries."

He smiled. "No thanks."

Micah sat down in a nearby chair.

Tamara's eyes traveled to the clock sitting on the mantel of the fireplace. "Micah, you should probably get back to the club. Justice will be performing soon."

"Look Tamara, I would still like you to do the interview. Eat quickly."

"Are you sure about this?" Tamara wanted to know. "I'm not in the mood to go back and forth with you on this, Micah. I know things ended badly ten years ago and that's one of the reasons I've been trying to reach out to you. I had hoped that we'd talk so that I could try to make things right."

He nodded. "As you said earlier, this is not the time for a talk like that. But yes, I'm sure about the interview. Tamara, I want you to write the article."

She wiped her mouth on the edge of her napkin. "What about the tour? Will I still be allowed to go along?"

Micah nodded a second time.

When she caught him eying her fries, she said, "Just go on and eat some."

Standing up, Micah chuckled as he crossed the room in long strides. "I was trying hard to resist."

Tamara held out her hand. "Friends?"

"Let's see how tonight goes," Micah responded. He wasn't ready to let down the walls guarding his heart.

"Fair enough," she said quietly. Tamara concentrated on her dinner while Micah made several business calls.

When Tamara finished, she pushed away from the table. "I need to freshen up, and then I'll be ready to leave."

Micah watched her from across the room. Tamara was so beautiful, even more than he remembered. He just wasn't sure that he could trust her ever again. He had no idea the type of woman she had become.

Ten years was a long time ago, but the wound of Tamara's rejection was still fresh, almost as if it had just happened.

Get over it, Micah's heart urged.

Tamara was the only woman he had ever loved, and now she was back in his life. He had one of two choices. Micah could let her walk out of his life a second time or he could move forward and give Tamara a second chance.

Micah's words stung but more than that they filled Tamara with shame.

He had every right to be angry with her because her actions that night were cruel.

Tamara had considered him one of her best friends— yet she chose to believe a lie without even consulting him about it. How could she ever hope to make this up to him?

She brushed her teeth and then touched up her makeup and hair.

When Tamara walked out of the bathroom, Micah stood there eying her from head to toe. For a brief moment, his eyes brimmed with tenderness and passion.

"You look beautiful."

"Thank you."

He reached out and pulled her into his arms, surprising her. "We're friends, Tamara. That won't ever change." Micah paused a moment, then said, "I have to be honest with you. I haven't gotten over what you said to me ten years ago, but I never stopped caring about you. I won't deny that there were days I wished I didn't."

She hugged him back. "Micah, I never meant to hurt you."

He kissed her cheek. "We'll talk later. Now let's get going."

They left the suite and took the elevator down to the lobby.

On the way to the club, Micah told her, "Just so you know, I'm not trying to avoid a discussion with you. I know that we need to talk, Tamara."

She nodded and hid her trembling hands in the folds of her dress. "I just want a chance to explain what was going on back then."

"We'll do it before you go back to Atlanta," he promised. "There are some things I need to say to you, too."

"I hope you'll let me go first," Tamara stated.

He laughed and shook his head. "Some things never change."

She relaxed as the tension between them evaporated.

Micah and Tamara continued their light banter during the short drive back to the club, making it just minutes before Justice was due to perform.

Micah went backstage while she sat down across from Sunni.

"Oh you're back, I see," she commented drily when Tamara joined her at the table. "Where's Micah?"

"He went to check on Justice."

"You ran out of here in a hurry," Sunni stated. "What happened? Did you have a family emergency? A sick child?"

"No, I didn't," Tamara responded. "And I don't have any children."

Sunni's eyes strayed down to her left hand. "Oh, I just assumed you were married."

"Well, I'm afraid that you assumed wrong," Tamara retorted with a tiny smile.

"How well do you know Micah?" Sunni asked. "He mentioned that you were friends in college, but your friendship could not have been as close as you believed, especially since he never mentioned you to me. You won't believe all of the people coming out of the wood-work claiming some close relationship to Micah. We all know that it's because he's a celebrity."

Tamara held her temper in check. She was not going to let Sunni bait her into an argument. She had no idea what Micah saw in a woman like her.

Micah sat down in the empty chair between her and

Sunni. Tamara was glad to have him at the table. Maybe Sunni would keep her snide comments to herself in his presence.

She turned to face the stage, bobbing her head to the music. Justice was an amazing performer. Tamara made mental notes when he dedicated one of the songs to the memory of his mother and spoke of how much he missed her.

After the performance, Micah led Tamara backstage for a one-on-one interview with Justice.

While she talked with the performer, Micah quietly observed them in the background. Tamara could feel the heat of his gaze on her, causing her heart to hammer foolishly. She managed to finish the interview.

"So what did you think?" Tamara asked him.

"It was an interview," Micah commented. "I'll reserve judgment until I see what you put in print."

They walked outside of the club.

"I need to call a taxi," she stated.

"No," Micah replied. "I'll have my driver take you home. After I drop Sunni off I'll come to your suite unless you'd rather talk sometime tomorrow. However, you'll be leaving to join Justice on tour."

"Tonight's fine."

She rode in the limo with Micah and Sunni.

The woman had no shame, Tamara thought silently. Sunni was draped over him in such a possessive manner that she was tempted to laugh.

Tamara uttered a soft prayer of thanks when the limo pulled in front of her hotel. She didn't care for Sunni at all and couldn't figure out what Micah saw in the woman.

She took the elevator up to the sixteenth floor and into her suite. She surveyed her reflection in the mirror.

Micah returned to the hotel shortly after midnight.

"I wasn't sure I'd be seeing you again tonight." Tamara could not resist adding, "I was sure Sunni would try to keep you with her all night."

The beginning of a smile tipped the corners of his mouth. "I told you that we'd have our talk, Tamara. *I meant it.*"

They sat down on the sofa.

Tamara spoke first. "Micah, I owe you a huge apology for the things I said to you graduation night. I feel like I can't say sorry enough."

His closeness was so male, so bracing that she had to wrench herself from her preoccupation with his handsome face.

"Tamara, I accept your apology," he said in response.

"I was so messed up back then," she explained. "My life was crazy, Micah."

"It is what it is," he stated without emotion. "Tamara, there's really nothing that you can say now that will ever change what happened."

"You're still angry with me over it," she acknowledged. "Micah, I can tell by the way you're treating me. What I need to know is if we can ever get past what happened? I'm willing to try if you are."

A muscle quivered at his jaw. "Things changed between us that night, Tamara. I can't understand why you would believe something a bunch of guys told you. We had been friends since our freshman year at Hollington."

She shriveled a little at Micah's expression. "I know that, Micah," Tamara responded. "I eventually came to that conclusion but then I found out that it was just a nasty joke. I tried to contact you but you refused my calls."

"You'd have refused my calls if the situation had been reversed, Tamara, but then again, I never would have believed what somebody else told me. After four years, I figured I knew you pretty well."

Tamara agreed. "You're right. I should have known better, but Micah, my head wasn't in the right place. I was so focused on getting out of school and landing a job so that I could take care of myself."

"So you keep saying."

"Micah, back then it was hard for me to trust anybody."

He released a long sigh before saying, "I guess what it comes down to is that none of it really matters anymore."

Micah rose to his feet. "It's late, and you need to get some rest. I'll see you in the morning before you leave."

"I miss you, Micah," Tamara blurted. "I really miss our friendship."

He didn't respond.

Tamara met his gaze. "Will you please say something?"

"I don't know what you want me to say."

"That you miss our friendship as much as I do or that you want us to be friends again." She shrugged. "Something like that, maybe."

Micah drew his lips in thoughtfully. "I'll see you in the morning."

He was still guarded so Tamara didn't press him.

Instead, she walked Micah to the door and said, "I really appreciate this opportunity in spite of what happened between us. I just hope you will consider letting me back into your life."

Micah hugged her and then left the suite, leaving Tamara alone with her thoughts.

"I'm going to find a way to win back your trust," she whispered. "And your heart."

Chapter 5

Tamara was up early the next morning packing for the tour. She was so excited about the tour that she couldn't sleep. She ordered room service and had just enough time to eat a bagel with cream cheese and a couple of strawberries.

Tamara jumped at the sound of a loud knock on her bedroom door.

She walked briskly across the floor expectantly.

"I thought it might be you," she stated when Micah entered the suite. "I remember how punctual you used to be. I guess some things never change."

"And I recall that you were never ready whenever I arrived," he countered, looking around the suite. "Do you have everything packed and ready to go?"

Tamara broke into a smile. "Micah, you'll be

proud of me. I'm *almost* ready. Just need to pack up my computer."

"Some things never change," he said with a chuckle. "Did you sleep okay?"

"Not really," she responded. "But it's because I'm really looking forward to this tour. I'm sure I'll catch a nap at some point while we're on the bus."

Tamara packed her laptop and closed her tote. "Okay. I have everything."

Looking up as she approached, Micah openly studied her. Things were still a little tense between them but they were both attempting to be cordial.

"Did you eat any of your breakfast?" he inquired. "It looks untouched."

"I ate a bagel and some fruit. I don't know if you remember, but I'm not really a breakfast person."

"I remember," he stated. "I used to have to force you down to the dining hall every morning."

Tamara was touched that he remembered. He had warmed to her some since their talk, but Micah was still guarded at times.

They left the suite and took the elevator down to the lobby.

Tamara chewed on her bottom lip.

"Nervous?" Micah asked.

"I am," she confirmed. "I'm the outsider. I don't know how the band members are going to respond to me."

"You don't have to be nervous. Everyone is really down-to-earth. You'll see."

He drove her over to his office building where they were loading up the buses.

Following behind Micah, Tamara entered the first crew bus. She swiveled slowly, her delight growing.

"You'll be traveling on this one," he told her. "You will be sleeping in the executive suite located in the back of the bus—there's a double bed and a full bathroom. You'll also have your own TV and DVD player in the suite. The other TV is in the bunk area."

"Wow," Tamara murmured. "This is really nice, but where is Justice and everybody else sleeping? He should have the suite."

"There are eight bunks for the others. Justice will sleep in the suite on the other bus."

She surveyed her surroundings. The lounge area featured a leather sofa and two overstuffed chairs, a flat-screen LCD TV, DVD player, CD player and a surround sound system. Doors separated the bunk areas from the lounge.

The fully equipped kitchen came with a large fridge, coffeemaker, microwave and toaster.

"You will be able to get on the Internet if you need to," Micah said. "There is a collection of movies and PlayStation games available on board, as well."

"This tour bus is incredible," Tamara commented to Micah.

"I like for my artists to travel in style. You will be going to Seattle, Vancouver, Portland, San Francisco and then back here to Los Angeles. You'll fly out the day after the L.A. concert—I've already arranged for your ticket."

"Are you coming with us?"

Micah shook his head no. "Not on the bus," he responded. "I'll be flying to Seattle tomorrow for the concert."

"Oh, okay. I guess I'll see you then." Tamara had hoped they would be traveling together. She had so many questions for Micah.

She wanted to know what inspired him to start his record company, why he wasn't performing himself and how serious he and Sunni were. She and Micah had ten years to catch up on, but apparently, he was not as curious about her life.

She and Micah embraced before he departed the bus. "I'll see you tomorrow," he promised.

A couple of band members started up a game of chess while another played his PlayStation. One was sitting across from her in the lounge with his eyes closed, listening to his iPod device. Justice Kane was in the back of the bus talking to the road manager and one of the female background singers. He had decided to ride on this bus for the first leg of the trip.

Justice joined her a few minutes later.

She spent the morning listening to him and making notes as he talked about the effect music had on him and how it essentially saved his life.

"I went to Micah's store one day, and this music came on that really spoke to my spirit and I just started singing."

"Was this a song that you had written?" Tamara asked.

He shook his head no. "It just came to me. I could see the words in my mind. I know you think I'm tripping, but I'm not. I have never been able to remember any of that song since that day. I guess it was just meant for Micah's ears. We started working together after that."

"Is it true that he put up the money for your first album?"

"He sure did. I didn't have nothing but a police record. Micah told me that he would rather invest in my future than have me out there trying to steal the money for a demo. I ain't gon' lie—that's what I was gonna do. After that song, I was determined to get the money for my album by any means necessary, but you know what? It wouldn't have worked out this way."

"So how exactly did music save your life?" she asked him.

"It gave me a dream. Micah told me that God don't give you a vision without giving provision. I believed him."

"I read in *People* that you're very passionate about helping other young men get their lives together. What are you doing outside of the concerts to promote anti-gang activity and speaking in the schools?"

"I sponsor two Pop Warner football teams—one in the ATL and the other one in Los Angeles. I also have a college scholarship fund to send kids to college who may not be straight-A students but have the desire to better their lives. I'm considering building a boarding school for boys somewhere in the Midwest who really want out of the gang life. I want to put them in a safe environment, and the location will have to be kept quiet. I'm still working all that out, you know?"

"This is all very impressive."

He smiled. "Somebody held out a hand to me when I was out there. I have to pay it forward, you know? Do the same thing. Help others because everybody deserves a second chance."

She nodded in agreement.

Tamara made more notes as they discussed his new album.

When they stopped for lunch, Justice returned to his bus to take a nap.

She navigated to her own suite and shut the door to type up her notes.

Tamara liked to write while the story was fresh in her mind. She turned on her iPod handheld, stuck her earphones in and worked.

Three hours passed before she emerged from the suite to get bottled water from the fridge.

One of the background singers approached her.

"So how are you enjoying yourself so far?" she asked. "I'm Marty. I didn't get a chance to introduce myself earlier."

"Marty, it's nice to meet you. I'm Tamara. Things are going well. I love the bus."

"By the end of the week, you may not feel that way," she said with a chuckle.

"How long have you been touring with Justice?"

"About a year now," Marty responded. "He's my cousin. When I lost my job, he offered me this gig. I don't like being away so much from my family but it keeps a roof over our heads."

"How many children do you have?"

"Two. My son is almost five and my daughter is two. They're with my husband. He lost his job six months ago. He's in school trying to finish up his degree so that he'll be able to apply for some management positions."

"Marty, that's wonderful," Tamara stated. "But I'm sure it's hard with him in school and having young children."

"Thank the Lord for my mama. She watches them when I'm on the road and Terry's in class." Marty picked up an apple and bit into it. "Do you have any children?"

"I don't," she responded. "Maybe one day. Hopefully a husband will come before the baby."

"A woman as pretty as you won't have any problems in that department. I saw the way Micah was looking at you. You definitely have his attention."

Tamara smiled. "Micah and I have known each other for over ten years. We were best friends in college, but after graduation we lost touch with each other."

Marty became animated. "So this is the first time you two have seen each other since you graduated?"

She took a sip of water and nodded.

"That's so sweet," Marty murmured. "I love reunions of any kind. It's just something special about a coming together in unity."

"Would you like to watch a movie or something?" Tamara asked. "I have that huge suite to myself. We might as well enjoy it."

"Do you mind if I ask Yuri to join us?" Marty inquired, referring to the other female singer.

"That's fine. The more the merrier," Tamara responded. "Hopefully, the others won't think that we're antisocial."

Marty laughed. "Girl, they'll be thrilled that we're not out there trying to watch some chick flick or Lifetime. Yuri and I usually end up in the suite watching television most of the time."

"Oh, no…did I get you kicked out of the suite?" Tamara questioned. "I could sleep in one of the bunks."

"You don't want that, trust me." Marty took another bite into the apple. "I'ma go get Yuri. We'll be back there in a few minutes."

Tamara enjoyed spending time with the women. Marty and Yuri were very friendly and both possessed a wonderful sense of humor—something they stated was necessary when on the road.

They continued bonding over dinner. She listened in amusement as the women heaped praises on Micah about how thoughtful he was and how blessed Tamara was to have him as a friend.

That evening, she changed into a pair of shorts and a T-shirt for bed. After she pulled down the covers and climbed inside, Tamara pulled out her journal and began writing.

August 30

I can't believe that I'm actually on tour with Justice Kane—at least the West Coast leg of the tour. The crew and band have all been so nice and friendly. They've gone out of their way to make me feel welcomed.

I really thought that Micah and I would have some time to just talk but he's really a busy man. He's flying to Seattle tomorrow for the concert, but I'm sure Sunni will be with him so we may not have the chance to talk then, either.

I don't know how I know this, but that woman is not as nice as he thinks she is—when he wasn't around, she got in her share of digs but I simply ignored her. I didn't come out here for drama. I am not sure how I should feel about Micah never once mentioning me to her. I guess he must have really hated me.

At times, he seems like the person I used to

know but then other times he acts so distant. It's all my fault.

How could I have ever believed those boys? I should have known better—Micah had always been a perfect gentleman. I should have realized that when he professed his love for me it wasn't a ploy to get me into bed.

He had been speaking from the heart, and I rejected him in the cruelest way possible.

The next day Micah took an early morning flight to Seattle.

He wanted to spend some quality time with Tamara before the concert. This was her first trip to Washington state, and he wanted to show her around the city.

Micah wavered between forgiveness and unforgiveness where she was concerned. Although Tamara had given him an explanation for her actions, he wasn't convinced it was for that reason alone. There was more that she wasn't telling him. Until he knew the truth, Micah was not sure that they could ever recapture the closeness they once shared.

Micah arranged to have his overnight bag delivered to his suite after checking in, then headed straight to see Tamara.

"I'm so glad you're here," she told him. "This city is beautiful. At least the little bit I've seen so far."

"While the others are in rehearsal, I thought I'd take you on a tour of the city," Micah announced. He smiled in that old familiar way that used to make her heart turn over.

The sound of her voice did things to Micah. Just

seeing her again nearly left him breathless. He sat down to try to hide his state of arousal. Micah tried to wrench himself away from his thoughts of Tamara in various states of undress.

"You don't mind?" she asked, bringing him out of his reverie.

"Not at all. There are some places I'd like to show you."

"That would be great," she responded. "I'm dressed and ready for once." Dressed in a crisp white sleeveless shirt and a pair of walking shorts, Tamara was ready to tour Seattle.

"You might want to change your shoes. Those sandals are nice and fashionable, but I'm not sure they're going to be so comfortable."

Tamara gave him a sidelong glance. "So what should I wear?"

"A pair of tennis shoes," he suggested.

She smiled. "I have those. Give me a minute to change." Micah laughed.

"I was still ready," she uttered. "This doesn't count."

Tamara glanced down at her feet and said, "They don't go with my outfit. I think I need to change." She glanced up at him. "Don't you utter a word."

They left the suite thirty minutes later.

"Our first stop is going to be the Woodland Park Rose Garden," Micah told her. "I know how much you love roses. They have over two hundred sixty different types of roses." He further explained, "The garden is one of twenty-four All-America Rose Selections Test Gardens in the United States."

"I can't wait to see the different varieties. My mother

has been experimenting, trying to come up with a new hybrid tea rose."

"What about you?" Micah asked. "Are you still into gardening?"

Tamara shook her head no. "Not since my grand-mother died. I think that I loved it because I enjoyed being with her. Micah, I miss her so much."

She put a hand to her neck. "When I lost the neck-lace she gave to me…things just haven't been the same. It was really special, and I felt close to her when I had it."

Micah glanced over at her. "Your grandmother is in your heart. You do know that, don't you?" He remem-bered how upset Tamara had gotten when she realized it was gone. He vowed back then to find one like it because he knew how much that piece of jewelry meant to her.

"Yeah, I know, but it would be nice to have some-thing of hers to keep with me. That necklace always made me feel safe."

As soon as Tamara stepped out of the car, her sensi-tive nostrils caught the mixed fragrance of exotic roses. "It's so beautiful," she murmured as they entered the park.

"Am I allowed to take pictures?" she asked. "My mother would love to see this."

"You can take as many photographs as possible."

Micah reached over and took her hand, leading her along the winding paths and through soft bright green grass. There were hundreds of explosions of bright colorful blooms everywhere.

Tamara enjoyed the feel of his skin touching hers. It

had been a long time since they walked anywhere holding hands like this.

"This reminds me of old times," she confessed, savoring his touch.

Micah smiled but did not respond.

She was touched that he remembered her love for roses and brought her to Woodland Park. Tamara felt like they were reconnecting finally. Maybe now he would let down the wall guarding his heart.

Tamara released his hand to take several digital photos to e-mail to her mother when she got back to the hotel.

"Do people get married out here?" she asked.

Micah nodded before responding, "All the time."

"I can see why. It's so romantic."

"Yeah, it is," Micah agreed, his eyes focused on Tamara's face. "Being surrounded by so much beauty."

Tamara shivered a little from the way Micah was staring at her. She loved him so much, but now was not the time to make that declaration. She did not want to scare Micah away.

They walked through the entire park, stopping every now and then for Tamara to get a closer look or inhale the fragrance of a particular hybrid.

"Micah, you've got to smell it," she stated. "It has a very exotic scent."

He bent down and sniffed. "You're right."

His face was so close to hers. Tamara tried to slow her racing heart as she straightened up her body.

"You okay?" Micah inquired.

She nodded. "I'm fine."

Tamara took more photographs. "My mom is going to love these pictures."

"I'm glad you're having a good time."

"Micah, I am," Tamara confirmed. "Thanks for bringing me here."

Deep down, she was thrilled to have this time alone with Micah. If she were going to win back his friendship, they needed to become reacquainted with each other.

"So where are you taking me now?" Tamara questioned as they headed back down to the car. She was really enjoying herself and prayed that Micah felt the same way.

"To Snoqualmie Falls," Micah answered. "Have you ever heard of it?"

"Yeah," Tamara uttered. "I've heard that the Falls are unbelievable. I can't wait to see it for myself."

They made small talk during the drive. Tamara did not want to push Micah too hard. She knew that he needed a chance to feel comfortable around her.

Micah and Tamara walked along the paths through the two-acre park hand in hand listening to the roar of the whitewater as it tumbled over granite cliffs.

Tamara noticed that there were several secluded picnic areas—perfect surroundings to share a romantic lunch.

They strolled along the tree-lined trail, and then went up to the gazebo inspired observation deck so that Tamara could take pictures of the two hundred seventy foot waterfall.

"We used to always talk about traveling to Africa to see Victoria Falls," she reminded him. "Do you remember that?"

Micah nodded. "We had planned to go to Egypt, too. Remember? We talked about seeing the Pyramids of Giza and the Sphinx. We were going to travel the world."

She chuckled. "We made a lot of plans, didn't we?"

A strange, faintly eager look flashed in his eyes. "Yeah, we did."

"Did you ever go?"

Micah glanced over at her. "Where?"

"To Egypt," Tamara replied. "I read somewhere that you went to Africa. You supplied several schools with computers."

"*Ebony* did a big article on that," he responded. "But to answer your question, I haven't gone to Egypt. In all honestly, I guess I was waiting on you."

"Micah, we should go," Tamara blurted. "Not this year but next summer. What do you think?"

"I don't know that we're ready to take trips together, Tamara. We still have a lot to work through, so let's not get ahead of ourselves. Let's just take this one day at a time," Micah said with quiet emphasis.

"Of course," Tamara murmured. She was thrown by the coolness in Micah's tone. There was no warmth in his words.

I'll just have to work that much harder to get him to trust me again, Tamara decided. Theirs was a friendship worth saving.

After taking in all that the park offered, Micah and Tamara ventured to The Falls Gift Shop. They paused to check out some of the memorabilia. Tamara purchased a few items for Kyra, her sister and her mother.

Micah hadn't said much since they left the shop, but he warmed up a little by the time they sat down to have lunch. He was more himself then.

They enjoyed burgers and shakes at the Snoqualmie Falls Candy Factory while watching candy being made.

"This is so cool," Tamara whispered. "I haven't had this much fun in a long time."

Her words amused Micah. "You need to get out more."

She gave him a gentle jab with her elbow. "Stop being so mean."

"I'm just saying…"

"I have a life, I'll have you know," Tamara said with a chuckle. "I've learned to enjoy going to dinner alone, going to the movies and I even take in a few NFL and NBA games."

"Okay, then what you need is a man."

"Now you sound like Mama," she uttered. "That woman is always trying to hook me up with somebody. I think her friends are starting to keep their single sons hidden away."

Tamara and Micah laughed.

"My mom was like that before she died. She wanted me to get married and settle down," he said.

"How long has she been gone?" Tamara asked. She had met Micah's mother shortly after he began tutoring her. She was a very religious woman who had little patience for nonsense. A college education was very important to her and she constantly reminded Micah to stay focused.

"Four years now." Micah shook his head regretfully. "She wanted me to find you. My mom always said that you were the one for me."

"My grandmother used to tell me the same thing," Tamara confessed.

For dessert, they shared a bag of caramel corn.

"I can't hang with you," Micah stated. "I haven't eaten this much junk food since college."

Tamara folded her arms across her chest. "Oh, so now I'm bad for your health?"

He laughed. "Sweetheart, I didn't mean it that way."

"You've gotten mean in your old age," Tamara uttered. "We should probably head back to the hotel. I think you need a nap."

Their gazes locked, and both of them could see the attraction mirrored in the other's eyes.

Micah pulled her into his arms. "A nap is the last thing I need right now."

The prolonged anticipation of kissing her had become unbearable. His mouth covered hers hungrily.

Raising his mouth from hers, Micah gazed into her eyes.

Tamara drew his face to hers in a renewed embrace. He kissed her again, lingering, savoring every moment.

"What are we doing?" Micah whispered. He marveled at the soft, satiny texture of her skin. He knew that Tamara would feel as good as she looked. He had seen breathtaking women from all over the world, but the woman standing with him possessed an unrivaled beauty.

Tamara had it all as far as Micah was concerned. She had it all—perfect features, silky flesh, a refined bone structure and a beautiful head of hair.

But could he trust her with his heart?

Tamara's emotions whirled. Blood pounded in her brain, leapt from her heart and made her knees tremble. After fourteen years of knowing him, Micah had finally kissed her—and it had been everything she'd dreamed it would be.

He released her. "I'm sorry. I shouldn't have done that."

"Micah, you don't have to apologize for anything. This is something we both want," she stated, his apology darkening the moment.

"I have always been drawn to you, Tamara," he confessed. "As much as I've tried to fight my feelings, I can't stop thinking of you."

Her face clouded with uneasiness. "Are you complaining? Are you saying that you don't want to want me?"

"No, of course not," Micah replied. "I just want to make sure we're not rushing into anything. Our friendship is still too fragile."

There was a pensive shimmer in the shadow of his eye.

"I'm glad to hear that we still have some form of friendship. I was worried earlier," she said. "I don't want to keep looking back into the past, Micah. I've done that most of my life. I thought we were starting over."

"We are," he confirmed. "You're right, Tamara. We won't look back." Micah gathered her into his arms and held her snugly. "I have really missed you."

He touched his lips to hers.

Tamara kissed him with a hunger that belied her outward calm. She was shocked by her own eager response. She felt blissfully happy and fully alive.

They didn't linger any longer because they needed to head back to the hotel.

The concert was in less than three hours.

"I told you that you needed a nap," she teased as they got inside of the rental car.

"Actually, I was thinking that you might need to rest up before the concert," Micah retorted. "I know you can't hang like you used to."

"You're the same age as I am," she reminded him, enjoying the easy banter between them. "Besides, if I remember correctly...you were the one who used to get sleepy."

Micah laughed. "That was ten years ago, and back then I was the studious one, not the party animal."

Tamara tried to stifle a yawn, sending him into another round of laughter. She was struggling to keep from falling asleep during the ride back to the hotel, but she wasn't about to tell Micah that as soon as she returned to her suite she was taking a nap.

Her mind was still on Micah when she was alone in her hotel suite. A delicious quiver surged through her veins as Tamara recalled how much she had enjoyed his company.

"We had a nice time," she whispered to herself. "And he kissed me."

Tamara removed her clothes, showered and slipped on a pair of silk shorts with a matching top.

Restless and Micah dominating her thoughts, Tamara attempted to ignore the strange aching in her limbs.

"Micah, you're driving me crazy," she groaned. "I need to get you out of my head."

Tamara had a brief chat with her sister and her mother. As usual, she and Jillian had words over her mother's constant attempts to find a suitable husband for her.

Her mother had called to see when Tamara would be returning home. She wanted to host a dinner party and already had a date selected for her daughter. Only Tamara wasn't having it and told Jillian so.

Jillian also wanted minute-by-minute reports of her relationship with Micah. Tamara recalled when her mother could not stand the thought of her daughter spending time with someone like Micah—a kid from the projects who attended college on an academic scholarship.

On the other hand, Tamara's grandmother adored him. Now that he was a powerful and wealthy executive, Jillian suddenly had a change of heart where Micah was concerned. Her mother was not born into wealth so she was determined to marry well and wanted the same for her daughters.

Tamara loved her mother but wished deep down that Jillian wasn't so motivated by money. The woman would sell her soul for a million dollars.

Alone in his suite, Micah was enraptured by the vision of Tamara in his mind and was beside himself with want.

He strode into the bathroom and turned the cold water on full blast. After removing his clothes, he stepped beneath the freezing spray of water.

Micah welcomed the cold and painful comfort in an attempt to cool his ardor. However, the water did very little to lessen his desire that Tamara had aroused. He kept thinking of the heated kisses they had shared and how she'd responded to him.

He towel-dried his shivering body ten minutes later.

A still-frustrated Micah walked quietly out of the bathroom and padded barefoot into the living room. He sat down at the desk and called Bette, his secretary, to check in.

Work would keep his mind off his thoughts of Tamara.

He turned on his laptop and responded to the e-mails he deemed priority. Fleeting images of Tamara crept into his head now and again, but Micah forced them away.

An hour later, he was still unable to focus on his work. Micah hoped that Tamara was having just as hard a time keeping her thoughts off him.

Tamara and Micah returned to the Alexis Hotel after Justice's concert at Key Arena. Despite the late hour, Micah wasn't ready for the evening to end. He invited her up to his suite. Tamara did not know it, but Micah had arranged for a private catered late dinner to be delivered to the suite.

"Is this where you usually stay when you're here in Seattle?" she asked, following Micah inside the room.

He nodded. "Why do you ask?"

Tamara sat down on the sofa and crossed her legs. "They seemed to know you at the front desk." She gave him a sidelong glance. "I bet I know why you like this place so much."

"Why?"

"Because of the restaurant," Tamara responded, referring to the Library Bistro & Bookstore Bar. "I took a peek inside when I arrived. I really love those high-back booths and the tall bookcases."

Micah sat down in one of the overstuffed chairs. "I admit that I do enjoy the ambiance. The food's not bad, either."

"I wouldn't know," she replied. "I haven't eaten there yet."

There was a knock on the door of his suite.

Tamara glanced over at Micah. "Are you expecting someone?" She fervently hoped that Sunni hadn't decided to surprise him. Tamara was not one for drama, so she hoped there wasn't going to be any.

She and Micah had not really discussed his relationship with the model because Tamara was hesitant to
bring up the subject.

He got up and nodded as he crossed the room.

Micah opened the door to allow the waiter to enter,
pushing a cart laden with food. He worked quickly,
covering the table with a white tablecloth.

She rose to her feet, moving to stand beside him.

Tamara's smile widened in approval. "Wow. You
sure are full of surprises."

"I know how much you like to eat," Micah teased.
He gave her body a raking gaze, lazily appraising her.

She elbowed him in the arm as they silently observed
the waiter placing their dinner on the table. "So what
are we having?" Tamara whispered.

Micah took her by the hand and led her to the table.
"For starters, we're having seared scallops with bacon,
mushrooms on baby lettuce, seared ahi tuna for our
entrée and for dessert, your choice of a lemon or almond
pear tart."

Tamara rubbed her hands together. "Sounds delicious."

Micah signed the check and gave the waiter a fifty-
dollar tip.

They sat down at the dining table to eat.

He quickly blessed the food before they dived in.
Tamara could feel him watching her. "Shouldn't you be
concentrating on your food?"

"I can't believe we're here like this," he confessed.
Micah's eyes traveled over her face and then slid downward. "Frankly, I never thought I'd see you again. I'm
glad I was wrong."

"I'm glad, too. I always believed that we'd see each

other again—I just didn't think it would take this long." Tamara wiped her mouth with the edge of her napkin. "It probably wouldn't have if you hadn't stayed out of my life."

"I didn't know what I wanted or how I wanted to handle it. I needed time, I guess." He stuck a forkful of food into his mouth and chewed slowly.

Tamara took a sip of her ice water. "Micah, if you had returned at least one of my phone calls, we could've gotten all this straightened out a long time ago."

He agreed. "Maybe, but I wasn't ready to talk to you then."

"We've had so much fun today, but I can feel that you're holding back. Micah, I'm not out here to hurt you. You *can* trust me. I want you to know that."

The air around them suddenly seemed electrified.

Tamara picked up the coffee pot and poured a cup for herself.

"We agreed not to look back anymore," she told him. "Didn't we?"

Sipping her coffee, she stared back out the glass patio doors, quietly observing the Seattle nightlife.

Taking her hand in his, Micah nodded. "You're right. I'm sorry."

She looked up into the face that God had lovingly created. Tamara had dreamed of his muscular body brushing against hers, the sensuous feel of his sinewy arms wrapped around her.

He cut into her thoughts. "Is something wrong with your food?"

Tamara felt the heat rise to her cheeks. "Oh, no…everything is fine."

I've got to stop thinking about this man like this. It had been a while since she was intimate with a man and she was human, Tamara reasoned silently.

After they finished eating, she pushed away from the table and stood up. "Dinner was delicious," Tamara murmured. "Now I have to go to my room and put together some notes for the article."

Micah kissed her, sending waves of shock through her body. Tamara had certainly not expected him to do this.

She pulled away slowly. "We also agreed to take whatever this is very slow. I actually do have some work I need to finish, and I need to make sure I'm ready when the crew buses pull out."

All evening, the tantalizing picture Tamara represented distracted Micah. Her lips, slightly parted, were full and generous, turning up at the corners in a perpetual smile. He visually traced the shape of her mouth with his eyes. A smile played across his lips as he recalled what hers felt like against his own.

"You're sure that's what you want to do?" he inquired hoarsely. "You really want to leave?"

"Micah, it's not that I want to leave," Tamara admitted. "I just think that it's the right thing to do."

He watched beneath hooded lids as Tamara drew back to study him. Micah wanted to beg her to stay but resisted the urge. "I guess I'll see you in the morning then."

They embraced.

"Good night," she said with her voice barely above a whisper.

"Let me walk you to your room." A shiver of wanting

ran down Micah's spine. He moved toward her, impelled involuntarily by his own passion.

Tamara shook her head. "I'm pretty sure that I can make it across the hall by myself," she told him with a chuckle. "If you walk me over there, I know that I won't be strong enough to make you come back to your own room."

"You're worried you won't be able to resist me?"

She grinned. "Actually, I was thinking that you wouldn't be able to keep your hands off me."

"You're probably right," Micah acknowledged.

"I'll see you in the morning."

When she left, Micah headed to the bathroom.

He was in desperate need of a cold shower. He found himself taking them often since Tamara was back into his life.

Chapter 6

Over breakfast, Micah announced, "I won't be joining you in Vancouver. I have to return to L.A."

"Oh, no," Tamara murmured. "I thought you'd be finishing out the rest of the tour with us." She finished off her cranberry juice.

Had she known that Micah was not coming on the tour, she might not have slept in her own suite last night. Tamara was looking forward to spending more time with him. They shared a connection that not even he could ignore.

She felt a certain sadness that their time together was ending. The buses would be pulling out within the hour. Her feelings for Micah were intensifying, and Tamara couldn't deny the spark of excitement at the prospect of a relationship with the love of her life.

"Micah, are you sure you can't come to Vancouver with us?" she asked when he escorted her to the bus.

"I have some meetings scheduled that I can't postpone. I'll see you in Portland."

He kissed her cheek and gave her a hug. "Get on your bus. You guys need to get out of here."

"See you in Oregon. Oh and just so you know…you owe me a real kiss when you get there." She knew how he felt about showing affection in public. Micah didn't want his relationships exploited over the tabloids and tried to keep as much of his private life private.

He smiled and nodded. "Bye, Tamara."

They were soon on their way, heading out of Seattle.

Tamara spent the first half of the ride in her suite working on her notes. She struggled to stay focused. Micah dominated her thoughts. *I have never wanted a man as much as I want him,* she thought.

When Tamara found that she couldn't concentrate on her work or rein in her emotions where Micah was concerned, she decided to call it a day. She picked up her journal and opened it.

September 1
Today Micah and I had a wonderful time in Seattle looking at all of the many different types of roses in Woodland Park. We had such a great time together that I really wish he were going to be with us for the next leg of the tour. The more I spend time with Micah, the more I find myself thinking about him.

I can't even write about the hot dreams I have of the two of us together—they will forever be ingrained in the recesses of my mind.

I'm crazy about this man, but I know that he has this wall around his heart. I have to find a way to get him to give me another chance. I know that he has Sunni in his life and I'll respect that. Although I have to admit that I wish she wasn't around.

At least I'll see him in Portland. I think that the more time we spend together the more Micah will begin to trust me.

I'll write more later.

When Tamara arrived in Portland, Oregon, three hours later, she checked into the hotel and went straight to her room.

As soon as she unlocked the door to her suite, her eyes were drawn to the enormous bouquet of roses in vivid hues of pink, yellow, red and white. Tamara bent to inhale a whiff of the sweet fragrance.

She caught sight of the card attached and smiled as she read the note: "I'm really glad we're working on our friendship. I miss you already but I know that I'll be seeing you very soon. Micah."

"I miss you, too," she whispered as she stared at the lonely hotel bed.

When Justice and the band members headed out to Vancouver for rehearsal, Tamara went along with them. The concert was in Vancouver, which was less than twenty minutes away, and with the next concert being in Portland, it was easier to have them stay at one hotel for both nights.

Tamara made notes of her observations and conducted several interviews with the road manager, Marty and the drummer, Eric, who had been playing for various performers for over twenty years.

After rehearsal, they returned to the hotel so that Justice could get some rest before the concert that night. She and some of the band members gathered at a nearby restaurant to have lunch.

Micah called Tamara a few minutes after she arrived to her suite.

"How's it going?" he asked.

"Great," Tamara responded. "Thanks for the roses. Micah, they're gorgeous."

"I'm sorry I couldn't be there with you for the concert tonight, but I'll be in Portland tomorrow morning."

"I can't wait to see you," she confessed.

"Same here," Micah responded. "I have a meeting in fifteen minutes so I have to go but wanted to check in with you."

They hung up.

Tamara strolled over to the bed and sat down on the edge, clutching a pillow to her. Her eyes traveled back over to the vivid display of roses. They were really breathtaking and red roses were her favorite, but there was no romantic meaning behind them—Micah had made that clear in his note.

She sat there like that for nearly thirty minutes, wondering how to make Micah fall in love with her.

Portland, Oregon

It had been a long night.

After the concert in Vancouver, Tamara went back to the hotel. Marty and the others invited her to go clubbing with them, but she begged off. Instead, she spent her evening watching television.

Sleep did not come easy for her, mostly because Micah dominated her dreams. Tamara believed it was because of the anticipation of her need for physical intimacy. As much as she tried to ignore the truth, it was there. She wanted Micah to make love to her.

Micah called her again last night, but they did not talk on the phone that long. He only wanted to make sure things were going well with her and Justice Kane.

Tamara woke up several times during the night, and finally at 6:45 a.m., she got up.

She worked on her article until room service delivered her breakfast.

When she finished eating, Tamara showered and put twists into her hair.

Every so often, she would check the clock. Micah's plane was scheduled to land at 10:05 a.m. Tamara was really looking forward to seeing him.

She swung open the door to her suite and into Micah's arms two and a half hours later.

His lips pressed against hers and then gently covered her mouth.

His masterful kiss turned her legs into jelly as tantalizing tremors undulated through Tamara. She never believed it possible to derive so much pleasure from merely kissing a man.

Micah's lips brushed against hers as she spoke. "You're the man who's been dominating my dreams at night. You know that, don't you? I'm glad that you're here, Mr. Ross."

"I'm actually happy to be here, too." After a brief pause, he added, "More than I thought I would be."

"So does that mean you really really missed me?" she asked with a chuckle.

Their eyes met and held.

"More than you can imagine," he told her.

Micah broke their lust-filled trance by saying, "Any idea what you want to see in Portland?"

Tamara nodded. "Rose City Park. It sounds like it's similar to Woodland Park Rose Garden in Seattle."

"It is," he affirmed.

They left the hotel in a rental car.

"You seem to know your way around this place," Tamara stated. "How often do you come here?"

Micah laughed. "A GPS system is a wonderful thing."

When they arrived at Rose City Park, Tamara picked up a brochure for the self-guided tour.

"Micah, according to this pamphlet, there are over six thousand, eight hundred rosebushes that present over five hundred varieties," Tamara stated. "This is Rose City."

He took pictures with her digital camera.

"The next stop is the Royal Rosarian Garden," she announced as they followed the brick path around the garden. "The brochure says that Royal Rosarians are ambassadors of goodwill for the city. They participate in many festivals throughout the Northwest and plant a rose at each site. A rose was planted for each prime minister."

Micah and Tamara completed their tour and ate lunch at a nearby restaurant.

"Where to now?" she questioned when they finished eating.

"The Japanese Gardens aren't too far from here," he told her.

Tamara found the walk uphill from the parking lot

to the garden somewhat steep. Micah grabbed her hand and led her up to the top where they saw a set of stairs.

"Okay, I'm working off my lunch today," she murmured with a short laugh.

Five separate gardens made up the Portland Japanese Garden. Tamara snapped pictures of Micah strolling along the pond garden. He took pictures of her with the tea garden as a beautiful backdrop.

A couple nearby offered to photograph them together in the natural garden.

"We look like lovers," Tamara told him when they reviewed the photo on camera.

Micah nodded in agreement.

She gave him a sidelong glance. "Does it bother you?"

"No," he responded. "Because we know the truth."

Tamara stopped walking. "So are you saying that you don't want to be my lover?" She folded her arms across her chest.

Micah laughed. "Sweetheart, I'd be lying if I said that."

She grinned. "Just checking."

He pulled Tamara into his arms, holding her close.

"What's gotten into you?" Tamara asked. "You are not the type of man who is openly affectionate."

Micah gave her a tender look. "You're right, which is why this should convince you of how much I really care about you, sweetheart."

She cleared her throat, pretending not to be affected by his words.

In a surprise move, Micah covered her lips with his in the middle of the garden.

Tamara put her arms around his neck, giving herself freely to the passion of his kiss.

"Wow…" she murmured as they parted.

He smiled. "Would you like to see the rest of the garden? We still have the stone and the flat gardens to explore."

She nodded.

Tamara and Micah made it back to the hotel shortly after four.

She lay down to take a nap before she had to meet him for dinner. Tonight they were planning to attend the after party and would be out late.

Tamara believed that Micah was beginning to trust her again and it thrilled her. Their friendship was still on the mend, but she sensed that it was also changing. She had strong feelings for him and from that kiss that Micah laid on her earlier she felt conflicted. There were times she was almost positive that he returned her affection, but then other times, Micah acted like there was nothing more between them than friendship.

Perhaps Micah was acting this way because of his relationship with Sunni, Tamara decided and made a mental note to ask him about his relationship with the model. If they were involved, then there was no place in his life for her.

As much as it would break her heart, Tamara knew she would have to move on with her life.

"Would you like to dance?" Micah asked her. They came over with the band and Justice Kane for the concert after party at a local club in downtown Portland.

She nodded. "I love dancing. I just haven't done it in a long time."

Micah eyed her in amazement. "What? Not the party animal herself…"

"Ha-ha…" she muttered, taking him by the hand. "I hope you've learned something other than that two-step you used to do."

Micah pretended to be offended. "I know you're not talking about me. Girl, I was too cool back then."

Tamara stood up, waiting for him to escort her to the dance floor. She walked slowly, her body swaying to the music. "This is my song."

He took her to the middle of the front of the dance floor and began dancing to the music. One song ended and another began while they were still on the dance floor.

Justice Kane tapped Micah on the shoulder. "Hey man, can I dance with the pretty lady?"

Marty sashayed toward them. "Tamara, I'll take Micah off your hands. I *love* this song."

Some of the partygoers stopped dancing to take pictures of Justice.

"This is the part of my life that I'm not feeling," he told Tamara. "The lack of privacy. Sometimes I just want to leave my house and just kick it with my boys or my girl, you know?"

Tamara broke into a smile. "The price of fame, huh."

He nodded. "But you know what? I'ma have to just deal with it. I wouldn't be Justice Kane if it wasn't for these people. I can't forget that."

"It's a nice way of looking at it," Tamara responded. "It shows that you appreciate your fans—that's what will keep them buying your albums. Besides the wonderful songs you sing, anyway."

When the music stopped, Justice escorted her back

to the table in the VIP lounge of Avalanche, a hot, hip new club. Micah was talking to the cocktail server when they arrived.

"I just ordered you a glass of white wine," he told Tamara.

She met his gaze and smiled. "Thanks."

They sat down.

"You look like you're having a good time," he stated.

"I am," Tamara confirmed. "I have to share this with you, Micah. I'm not trying to sound corny, but the best times of my life were when I was at Hollington College, with my grandmother and with you."

Micah shook his head in denial.

"It's true," Tamara insisted. "You didn't just teach me math—you taught me how to hope. When you used to tell me about the things you went through growing up, Micah, you were always so optimistic. I wanted that kind of peace. That same kind of hope for the future."

"Each day that we wake up is another chance for to better our lives. We only have to keep our heads to the sky." Micah reached over and took her hand in his. "Tamara, it's been great seeing you again. I feel like I'm getting my best friend back."

"I'm glad you said that," she murmured. "Because I feel the exact same way."

"I know that we're not looking to the past, but Tamara, I hope there's no hidden agenda here." He was not ready to tell her how he really felt about her because he was not a hundred percent sure of her motives. Micah had allowed her entry back into his life but until he knew that Tamara was legit—he would keep his heart protected at all costs.

It wasn't always easy to keep his emotions under control. Micah wanted Tamara in a way that he never wanted another woman. Whenever they were together, he found it difficult to keep his hands and his lips off her. Micah hoped that he wasn't sending her mixed signals but it was too soon to let down his guard.

San Francisco, California

Micah rode with Tamara on the crew bus for the ten-hour drive from Portland to San Francisco.

She was willing to give up the executive suite, but Micah would not hear of it. He insisted on bunking with the crew if he needed to rest.

He knocked on the door before sticking his head inside. "Busy?"

Tamara shook her head no. "What's up?"

"We're about to play spades," Micah announced. "Interested in playing?"

"Sure," Tamara responded. "I haven't played in a while."

"It'll come back to you."

For the next hour, they played as partners, winning all but one round.

They didn't arrive in San Francisco until after three.

"How is the article coming along?" Micah asked.

They checked into the hotel almost an hour ago and were now sitting around the pool.

"I have so much material for my article," she told him. "Micah, I think I'm going to have to break it up and do a series. At least that's the way I'm going to pitch it to my editor."

His BlackBerry handheld started to vibrate.

"I need to take this call," Micah announced, excusing himself. "I'll be back in a few minutes."

When he left, Marty ran over and sat down in the lounge chair he had just vacated. "I know it's not my business, but something's jumping off between you and Micah. Girl, I'm happy for you. Micah Ross is *fine*."

Tamara broke into a grin. "Really, we're just friends, Marty."

She shook her head in denial. "What he and Sunni are—that's friends. When Micah looks at you, it's like a man in love."

Tamara smiled but did not respond. She was not about to say anything about their relationship. If Micah wanted his people to know anything, he would have to be the one to tell them.

Marty rose to her feet when she saw Micah coming in their direction. "I know what I'm talking about." She winked, strolled off in her skimpy-looking bikini and jumped into the Olympic-size pool.

Tamara's cell phone started to ring. She saw that it was Kyra calling and answered it. "Hey, girl. What's up?"

"Nothing," Kyra answered. "I was calling to see how things are going on your trip. Are you and Micah having a good time?"

"We are," Tamara responded. She gave Kyra a quick rundown of the tour and her time spent with Micah.

They chatted for a few minutes more.

"I just got off the phone with Kyra," Tamara announced. "She told me to tell you hello."

"I haven't seen her in a while," Micah said with a

smile. "I saw Chloe once, but the only person I talk to on the regular is Kevin."

"Are you planning to come to homecoming this year?" Tamara asked. "It hasn't been the same without you."

"I've been thinking about it." Micah checked his cell phone one more time before laying it down on the glass table between them. "Justice will be performing so I might show up."

"Micah, I hope you'll come," Tamara commented. "I have really missed you not being in my life. This week has been wonderful but I want our friendship back. When you're in Atlanta, I expect to get a phone call, dinner or something."

"How about you cook me dinner?" he suggested. "Oh yeah…you can't cook."

"See, you don't know anything," Tamara shot back. "I am a pretty good cook. I took cooking classes."

He laughed. "What can you cook?"

"Everything," she stated. "I have an impressive collection of cookbooks."

He was watching her so intently that she asked, "Why are you staring at me like that?"

"You have no idea how badly I want to kiss you."

She felt her skin become flushed and heated. "It wouldn't bother me if you did."

Just then, a photographer snapped a picture of them.

Micah released a sigh of frustration. "Are you ready to go upstairs?" he asked.

She nodded.

"I wish people could get a glimpse of the man that I see," Tamara said in a low voice. They were inside the hotel waiting for the elevator doors to open.

"I know this is a part of the life I choose, but there are some things that I feel should be left private."

"I agree with you," Tamara stated. "I think you need to address this with the media. By not talking, they are left to form their own opinions, but if you put it out there they will know how you feel about it."

Micah seemed to be considering her words. "I haven't thought about it in that way."

"Just think about it."

She and Micah were alone during the ride up to the twelfth floor. He reached for her. "I'll take that kiss now."

Tamara leaned into his embrace.

"There's something I need to ask you," Tamara said, stepping away from him. "What exactly is your relationship with Sunni?"

"We are nothing more than friends. We hang out but we're not a couple—that's just the media's spin on it."

Tamara gave him a look. "Does she know this?"

"Why?" Micah asked. "What did she say to you?"

"She didn't really say anything to me, but it's pretty obvious to me that Sunni's in love with you. I can tell by the way she looks at you."

"Tamara, I've been very honest with her," Micah stated. "I don't know what else I can do. She knows that we are friends. Now let me ask you something—does my friendship with Sunni bother you?"

"Yeah, it does," Tamara confessed. "I'm not real crazy about the woman."

He laughed. "A lot of women feel the same way about Sunni. I have no idea why."

"Yeah, right," she grunted.

"We haven't really talked about your love life,"

Micah stated. "What's up with you? Do I have to worry about some man coming to break my nose?"

Tamara shook her head. "For some reason, I can't seem to find a man who isn't interested in anything other than money, social standing and sex. I'm to the point that I need to run complete credit, criminal and health background checks on a person before I go on a date with him. My sister just got married two weeks ago and so you know my mama." She stared up at him. "Why haven't you gotten married? I've always thought of you as the marrying type—a family man."

"I guess Miss Right just hasn't come along."

Tamara grinned. "So are you saying that Sunni isn't the one?"

He chuckled. "I told you already that Sunni and I are just friends although she is convinced that she's the right woman for me."

"I'm not surprised," Tamara uttered. "It's obvious that Sunni truly believes her own press."

Micah had to agree. "She has a good heart though."

"I'm not saying she's not a good person. She just likes herself a lot."

He laughed.

Chapter 7

The crew buses arrived back in Los Angeles a couple of hours ago.

Micah invited Tamara to spend the following week at his house. Neither one of them was looking forward to their time together ending.

"Well, you have your interview," Micah stated.

"Yeah, I do," she responded, sitting on the passenger side of his BMW X5 luxury SUV. "Thank you so much for the opportunity." She chewed on her bottom lip a moment before saying, "Micah, I've been thinking about something—another feature for the magazine. I have a huge favor to ask."

He glanced in her direction. "What is it?"

"I really want to be a feature writer with *Luster* magazine and this article on Justice Kane was my trial run, but if you would allow me to do an exclusive feature on you, that would seal the position for me."

The car was filled with a pregnant silence.

Tamara began to consider that she had crossed some imaginary line until Micah told her, "If you want to interview me, that's fine. Since you're spending this week with me—now would be a good time. I'm taking some time away from work."

"That's actually perfect, Micah. People want a chance to get to know the real you. They want to see you when you're not at the office." She broke into a smile. "Thanks, Micah. I owe you big time for this."

"You don't owe me anything. You know I'm only agreeing to do this because it's you, Tamara."

She could tell that Micah was not totally comfortable with the idea even though he had agreed to do the interview. "I know and believe me, I don't take this lightly. I'll only write what you want in print."

September 5
I think Micah and I are finding our way finally! He agreed to let me interview him for the magazine. This is a big deal for me because he is an extremely private person.

I'm honored that he's allowing me this chance. I hope that while working on the project together, Micah and I can build a stronger foundation for our friendship. This is more important to me than the article.

Samantha is going to be thrilled when I tell her about this. She will probably try to feature Micah on the cover. I wouldn't mind having him grace my coffee table. Micah Ross is fine!

Micah and I have made great strides after all that happened in the past. I'm grateful to have him back in my life. Until we reconnected, I felt like there was a piece of me missing.

With Micah back in my life, I feel complete.

His heart thumping, Micah couldn't deny that Tamara was having a tremendous effect on him, because under normal circumstances, there was no way that he would have agreed to do an exclusive interview with anyone.

It was Micah's policy to avoid the media and public unless it was necessary. He was a very private man and refused to speak on his relationships or his family, but with Tamara, it seemed natural to open up to her. After all, he had known her for fourteen years.

"Just so you know, I won't be discussing Sunni or my family—just the record company and the artists. Tamara, is that understood?"

"Understood," she responded. "I'm really not out to exploit you, Micah. I hope you know that."

Micah really wanted to believe her, and he would unless Tamara showed him otherwise.

She could not seem to take her eyes off him, prompting Micah to ask, "What? Why are you looking at me like that?"

"You…you've changed from that shy little boy to this high-powered executive. I have to admit that I find that incredibly sexy."

"So when I was a geek I was what? Dog meat?"

"Of course not, Micah," Tamara interjected. "I've

always thought of you as sexy, but seeing you confident and secure like this is even more sexy."

Micah bit back a smile. Tamara had a wonderful sense of humor although she was more subdued when they were in college. He loved seeing this new side of her. It was like getting to know her all over again.

An undeniable magnetism was building between them, forcing Micah to accept what he already knew. He still loved her. However, as strong as his feelings were for Tamara, Micah still erred on the side of caution. While they had made some progress toward the repairing of their relationship, there were things he still did not know about her.

Micah still had no idea why there seemed to be a shadow of sadness in her expression at times when she was not aware he was watching her. He had seen it many times when they were at Hollington College. She wanted to forget the past, but Tamara seemed haunted by something that happened to her a long time ago.

"What are you thinking about?"

He glanced over at Tamara. "It wasn't anything."

"Liar," she uttered. "Micah, you have always been a thinker. Something's on your mind, so spill it."

"I was thinking about how much I've enjoyed having you around. I'm glad you agreed to staying out here for another week. We still have a lot of catching up to do."

Micah hoped to unlock whatever she had been hiding all these years.

Chapter 8

Old insecurities set in, and Micah began to have second thoughts regarding his invitation. *Why did I invite Tamara to the house?* It might have been better for her to stay at the hotel, but it was too late now.

Tamara was not the type of woman who would be impressed by his wealth—she had grown up in the lap of luxury with the Devane millions. Her ex-stepfather owned Devane Industries along with several other companies.

He knew the answer. It was because Micah wanted some time alone with her—that was the truth of it.

Micah was afraid that he would not be able to get her out of his system. She was becoming too important to him. Deep down, that scared him.

He had opened his heart to Tamara once and she ripped it apart. Could he trust her this time? Could he allow her to get that close to him?

For Micah, the next week would be very telling as far as he was concerned. Before she left to go back to Atlanta, he would know for sure whether he could trust Tamara with his whole heart again.

He hoped that she wouldn't let him down a second time.

Sunni called him twice during the drive, but he let them go to voice mail. He would have a conversation with her later. If things worked out the way that he wanted with Tamara, he needed to make sure that Sunni understood her place in his life.

Micah had not objected in the past because he enjoyed her companionship, but things were about to change.

"You really have a beautiful house," Tamara complimented as they settled down in his huge family room. "Did you decorate or hire someone to do it for you?"

"I had some help," Micah admitted. "Decorating was your thing—not mine. My feet still hurt from your dragging me through all those model homes, furniture stores, estate sales and swap meets."

Tamara laughed. "We used to talk about the houses we would one day have." Her eyes traveled the room. "You have yours and then some. I have an apartment."

"You still live in midtown?"

She nodded. "The Plantation at Lenox."

"You don't live too far from me," Micah stated. "I have a house in Tuxedo Park."

"I love the homes over there," Tamara responded, lying back against the plush oversize pillows on his couch. "Micah, do you come to Atlanta often?"

"Actually, I do."

She was surprised. "Then why didn't you ever try to contact me?"

"I didn't know what to say to you," Micah confessed. "Like I told you before, I wasn't ready."

Tamara pulled at the fringe on her shirt as she talked. "I was so messed up back then. I had all this hurt inside of me that eventually turned into anger, and I took it out on you. Micah, if I could do this all over again—"

He shrugged nonchalantly. "There are no do overs in life, Tamara."

Awkwardly, she cleared her throat. "I know, but it doesn't stop me from wanting to erase the life I had and just start over again."

"You keep saying that, but Tamara, I just don't get what was so terrible about your life—I guess I'm missing something because from where I was sitting, your life didn't look bad at all."

"That's because you have no idea what was going on with me," she told Micah. "You don't have a clue."

He inched closer to her. "Sweetheart, I know that we promised not to revisit the past, but before we can really move forward, I think we're going to have to put everything on the table. What haven't you told me?"

Tamara stirred uneasily on the sofa. "We'll talk about that another time. I would rather not ruin our evening with the depressing story of my life. We haven't been together like this in such a long time. I want to just enjoy tonight."

Micah settled back against the couch. "Sure, if that's what you want to do."

"We *will* have that conversation. I promise."

"So besides Kyra, who else do you keep in contact

with from school? I remember how you and your sorors used to walk around like you owned Hollington College."

"I've seen Beverly a few times over the years," Tamara responded. "Remember her? She was the homecoming queen our senior year, but we don't really keep in touch. As for my sorors, we did not act like we owned the college," she pointed out. "The Pi Betas were always involved in some type of community service. That's what we were about." She gave him a sidelong glance. "Why didn't you ever pledge?"

"The whole fraternity thing just wasn't me," he responded. "I wanted to stay focused on my studies. My degree was my way out of the ghetto. I didn't need the distraction of a fraternity. I have nothing against them— they just weren't for me."

Throughout the evening, Tamara silently noted Micah's kindness to his staff.

When he showed her his office, the numerous public service awards on the walls impressed her. Now this same man once tutored and befriended her almost fifteen years ago.

"You've done so much for the city of Los Angeles," she murmured. "And Atlanta, too. Why don't you want people to know about it?"

"Because that isn't why I do it, Tamara. I don't want my donations to be about Micah Ross. God has blessed me so that I can be a blessing to others. This is what I really believe. The world doesn't need to know what I do or how I help other people."

"I know how much you value your privacy, Micah. I appreciate you sharing this part of your life with me.

I'm so proud of the man you've become." Tamara cracked a smile. "I even liked the man you were before."

"Would you like something to drink?" Micah asked as he rose to his feet. "I have iced tea, soda and bottled water."

"I'll take some tea," Tamara responded. "Thanks."

She was getting irritated with the way Micah ran hot and cold with her. Just when Tamara felt she was making some headway with him, his demeanor would turn cool. She was determined to break through that cement block he called a heart.

"This view is incredible," Tamara told Micah as they sat out on his balcony. "I could sit out here for hours just looking at the stars in the sky and at the city below."

Micah took a sip of his tea. "It's one of the reasons I bought the place."

Tamara rose to her feet and stood near the heavy railing. "Micah, what do you do when you're at home either here or in Atlanta?" she asked. "What is your day like?"

"I read, work out and sometimes I just lock myself in my studio and play the piano."

"Why don't you record your own music? You used to love it when we were in college."

"I like being in the background, Tamara. I've always been that way."

"But you have such a beautiful voice, Micah," she stated. "I think it's a shame to keep all of that talent hidden. This is what I want to write about—the things people would be surprised to know about Micah Ross."

He shrugged. "As far as I'm concerned, I just don't think there's a lot to say about me. Tamara, I don't think the interview should be about me. Why not focus the story on the record label?"

"Because our readers would be more interested in the man behind the company," Tamara responded. "Micah, don't you dare back out on me. You said you would do the interview."

He sighed. "Fine…I'll do it."

Tamara kissed him. "Thank you."

Micah wrapped an arm around her as they watched a movie on television.

She enjoyed being so close to him and drank in the comfort of his nearness.

"This is wonderful," she murmured. "Being together like this brings back some wonderful memories."

Fighting sleep, Tamara stretched and yawned.

"Uh huh…"

She glanced over at Micah. "Uh-huh *what?*"

"Didn't have your nap today?"

"Micah, you need to quit," Tamara uttered. "I can hang with the best of them. I don't know what you're talking about."

He laughed.

The telephone rang.

"I bet that's Sunni," she stated. "Maybe you should answer it. She wants to be your Mrs. Ross."

"That's never going to happen. I'm going to have a talk with her tomorrow," Micah announced. "There's no point in prolonging this."

"I thought you said that you two were just friends."

"We are, and I've told her that," he confirmed. "But I want to make sure that Sunni understands where I'm coming from. I know that she has feelings for me, but I've been nothing less than honest with her."

Later, Micah showed Tamara to the guest bedroom. "This is where you'll be sleeping."

"Great."

Tamara pulled the journal out of her purse before settling down in the queen-size bed to finish the entry she started earlier.

I'm spending the night at Micah's house in Beverly Hills. We've had a great time together just talking and getting to know each other all over again. I have missed my best friend terribly, and I'm so happy to have him back in my life.

I also remember how crazy I am about this man. I love him, and I think that he still has feelings for me. Sometimes I catch him staring at me, and it's a certain way that he looks at me—I can't really explain it.

I want to say something but since we are just beginning to reconnect, I am afraid to bring up the subject mainly because I don't want to scare him away.

I was a little disappointed when Micah told me that I'd be staying in one of the guest rooms. I actually thought we would…

We don't want to rush into anything so I guess I have to just keep my desire under wraps as if it were easy.

It's so hard. I have vivid dreams of Micah and me riding a wave of passion. I want him badly.

I really want this drought to come to an end.

There was a soft knock at the door.

"Come in," she called out as she quickly put her journal back into her purse.

Micah stuck his head inside the room. "I wanted to make sure that you were okay."

Tamara gave him a sexy smile. "To be honest, I'm not sleepy at all. I'm in the mood for another movie. What about you? You think you can stay up long enough to watch one?"

Micah got into bed with her. "I can't believe that you're still talking trash. You'll be the first one to fall asleep."

She laughed. "You're sure I'm not keeping you up, old man?" Tamara asked.

"I got your old man."

Tamara wrapped her arms around him, pulling him closer to her. She could feel his uneven breathing on her cheek, as he held her tightly.

Micah traced his fingertip across her lip causing Tamara's skin to tingle when he touched her. He paused to kiss her, sending currents of desire through her.

She caressed the strong tendons in the back of his neck.

"Make love to me," Tamara whispered between kisses. She was ready to take their relationship to the next level.

"You don't know how badly I've wanted to hear those words come out of your mouth," Micah confessed. "I've wanted you from the moment I saw you again."

"Then what are we waiting for?" she asked. "Ten years is long enough."

He bent his head and captured her lips in a demanding kiss.

Locking her hands behind his neck, Tamara returned his kiss, matching passion for passion.

Her ardor soaring, Tamara eased away from him and began unbuttoning her shirt.

Micah helped her undress. His breath seemed to catch when he glimpsed her in her underwear, the lavender lace bra and matching thong panties.

"You are so beautiful," he told her in a husky voice.

Micah undressed himself and joined her in the bed. His mouth covered hers again hungrily.

Tamara answered his kiss with a desire that belied her outward calm. Moaning, she drew herself closer to him as his hands explored her body. Fire burst through her arms and shoulders before spreading to her lower limbs. Sparks of pleasure shook her body.

Micah reached into the nightstand beside the bed and pulled out a condom before taking her as his own.

Tamara offered him her lips while offering her body, as well.

Their eyes met. Micah kissed her forehead, then returned his attention to her mouth. The kiss was hungry and fierce.

Together, their fulfillment came with an intensity that defied description. Micah and Tamara lay in a tangle, their chests rising and falling rapidly as they fought to recover from their fervid lovemaking.

Micah moved away from her, then asked, "Tamara, are you on the pill?"

"Why?" Tamara wanted to know, clutching at the damp sheets. "Why are you asking?"

"I think the condom broke." He released a short sigh. "I don't want you to worry though. I had an HIV test six months ago and it came back negative."

"I had one done about that time, too," Tamara stated. "I haven't been with anyone in over a year. To answer your question, I am on the pill."

"My last relationship ended six months ago," Micah declared. "Sunni and I aren't sleeping together."

Tamara gave him a sidelong glance. "Really? You two never once had sex?"

Shaking his head, Micah said, "No, because I didn't want to give her false hope."

She was secretly thrilled to hear that. "I don't have any regrets, if that's what you're wondering. I don't want to spend it talking about the past. What we just shared was very special. Micah, I never imagined it would be this wonderful between us so let's just focus on us."

"What exactly did you have in mind?"

Tamara kissed him. "Well, you're going to need another condom for that."

They made love once more before falling asleep, their bodies entwined in a lover's embrace.

Chapter 9

Micah had lain in bed awake long after Tamara had fallen asleep. He should've known this moment would come. He should have figured out long before now that they would have to define their relationship.

Having made love to Tamara, the time was now.

He did not want to hurt her—he knew what heart-break felt like and didn't relish going through it again.

"What are you thinking about?" she whispered, looking up at him and wearing a sexy grin on her face.

"You," he responded. "I have a confession to make, Tamara. I had planned to offer you the story on Justice Kane and then kill it to ruin your career, but deep down I could never do something like that to you. I couldn't because I—"

Micah stopped short of confessing his love for her.

He had made love to her with deep emotion but wasn't ready to give voice to those feelings yet.

"I'm really glad to hear you say that," Tamara said. She sat up in bed with her back pressed against a stack of pillows. "I love what I do, and my career means a lot to me. It's all that I have in my life right now."

He sat up beside her. "I admit that it was a childish thought," Micah stated. "I don't know why I ever considered doing something so petty."

"You were hurt," she told him. "And you wanted to hurt me back. Believe it or not, I understand what that feels like, Micah."

"We've come a long way to get to this point. All this time…"

"Wasted," Tamara finished for him. "We wasted ten years because of a simple misunderstanding." She turned in his arms, facing him.

"Putting my heart on the line isn't easy for me," Micah confessed.

"No more talking," Tamara whispered sleepily. "I just want to savor this moment."

She was snoring softly a few minutes later.

Micah woke up shortly after 7:00 a.m. the next morning.

He was still reeling from the amazing night he had spent with Tamara. Life was funny. You never had a clue if happiness was waiting around the corner or if it decided to show up ten years later. From Micah's perspective, she had definitely been worth the wait.

A smile spread across his face as he watched Tamara sleep. He planted tiny kisses on each cheek, her nose, her chin and her neck in an attempt to wake her up.

She moaned softly.

He placed a kiss on her lips.

Tamara opened her eyes, stretched and yawned. "Good morning."

She sat up in bed, pulling the covers up to hide her breasts.

Micah attempted to pull her down and into his arms, but Tamara moved out of his reach, leaning over to grab her purse.

"I was thinking that we could go on and get the interview out of the way?" she asked, slipping a tape into the recorder. "I know how uncomfortable you are about doing it."

Her words washed over him like a bucket of ice-cold water. Micah stiffened as realization dawned on him.

This had all been a ploy on Tamara's part. Apparently, the only reason she made love to him was because she wanted to interview him—Tamara cared nothing for him. She had taken advantage of him while they were in school, and she was still trying to make a fool of him now.

He had had enough. "I think I've revealed enough of myself to you already," Micah stated. "I can't believe I fell a second time for the same mess!"

Tamara wore a look of confusion. "I don't think I understand."

"Unfortunately, I do," Micah responded without looking at her. "Look, I have some phone calls to make. Bringing you here was a big mistake, so it'll be best if you leave."

"What is going on with you?" Tamara demanded, her voice trembling. "Why do you want me to leave?"

"Because you're no longer welcome in my house."

Speechless, Tamara climbed out of bed, picked up her clothing and rushed into the bathroom. She had no idea why Micah was suddenly so angry with her. Had this been part of his plan for revenge?

Micah had gotten out of bed and slipped on a robe when she walked out of the bathroom. "My driver will take you back to the hotel or where you want to go."

"Micah, what's wrong?" Tamara asked, her voice trembling. "What did I do to upset you this time?"

"I made the mistake of thinking that you were different from any other woman going after what she wants."

She replayed everything that happened in her mind. "Micah, I only thought you would want to get the interview out of the way so that you wouldn't have to dwell on it. You were relaxed and I thought you were comfortable with me. That's the only reason I suggested doing it this morning."

"It doesn't matter because you won't be getting your interview, Tamara." Micah's tone had become chilly.

"That's fine," Tamara said as she fought back tears. She didn't want Micah to see her cry. She would never give him that satisfaction. "It's pretty obvious to me that you're not the man that I thought you were, either. You can't seem to make up your mind whether to love me or punish me. You won't have to worry about me bothering you. *I get it now.*"

Tamara held her turbulent emotions inside until she was safely in the car.

She was confused by Micah's sudden chilly reaction this morning, especially after what they shared last night. Tamara had assumed that they had broken through all the ice surrounding his heart.

What happened between last night and this morning? He had totally misunderstood her attempt to put him at ease. If his intent was to follow through with hurting her, he accomplished what he'd set out to do. Micah's treatment wounded her to the core, but Tamara purposed in her heart to forget the memorable night she shared with him. It wasn't going to be easy, but in time it wouldn't hurt so much.

In time, she would forget.

Tamara booked herself into a hotel near the airport. She kept her outward calm until she reached the confines of her room. She unlocked the door, tossed her luggage to the side and navigated to the shower.

Beneath the running water, Tamara cried out her heartbreak in the shower. When she came out and dried her body and her face, Tamara gazed at her reflection in the mirror. She lifted her chin and felt a surge of determination and sheer willpower.

She could get through this, Tamara decided. She would do what she had been doing all of her life. She would survive.

Chapter 10

Tamara had been back in Atlanta for two days.

Her mother had called her at least three times since her return to check on her and invite her to lunch, which Tamara refused because she knew Jillian was most likely trying to play matchmaker.

She definitely was not interested in meeting another man. Her spirit was still low from Micah's rejection, so it was best that she be alone for now.

The telephone rang. Seeing that it was her mother again, Tamara answered it. "Hello, Mama." They had already spoken for a few minutes not even fifteen minutes ago. Tamara couldn't imagine what she wanted now.

"I'm thinking of making a nice dinner on Sunday," Jillian announced. "I hope you're free."

"Who else did you invite?" Tamara wanted to know. "Mama, I'm not in the mood for your matchmaking."

"I invited your sister and Bryant to join us. I thought it would be nice to have my family surrounding me."

"They haven't been married all that long, Mama. Callie and her husband might want to spend time alone," Tamara responded. "I'll come over, and we can cook a great meal for the two of us. It'll be fun."

"Honey, what's wrong?" her mother asked. "You haven't sounded like yourself since you came home from California. How did things go out there?"

"I got the information I needed for my story on Justice Kane. I'm almost finished with the last piece of the series."

"Did you and Micah get a chance to catch up?"

"We spent a couple days together," Tamara stated without emotion. "He seems to stay busy, but I'm not surprised. Micah has always been extremely focused."

"What was it like seeing him again?" Jillian inquired as casually as she could manage, but she did not have her daughter fooled for one minute.

"It was nice," Tamara answered. "Mama, please quit with all of the questions. This was a business trip. Not a romantic getaway."

"You mean to tell me that you and Micah spent your entire trip talking about business? I can't believe that he is that committed to Sunshine or whatever her name?"

Tamara chewed on her bottom lip to keep from smiling. "Mama..."

"I'm just saying," Jillian countered. "I know how much that boy cared for you when you were in school.

It was pretty clear to me that Micah was in love with you, Tamara."

"Well, he's not anymore," she responded. "Micah has moved on with his life, and I'm doing the same."

Her mother was not about to let her off the hook. That just was not Jillian's style. "Then why do you sound so sad if that's the case? Honestly, dear, you sound as if you've lost your best friend."

She wasn't about to confide in her mother, so she said, "Mama, can we please change the subject? I don't want to talk about Micah anymore."

"Tamara, you know that I'm here if you want to talk about anything. You don't have to keep your feelings all bottled up inside."

"Thanks," she muttered. "Mama, I just have a lot on my mind right now. I have to come up with some ideas to pitch to Samantha tomorrow."

"Are you enjoying your new position at the magazine?"

"I am," Tamara admitted. It was the only thing in her life that gave her joy now.

After promising to have dinner with her mother on Sunday, they ended their conversation. She hung up the phone and stretched out on her sofa, hoping her headache would disappear.

Micah was so angry he was trembling. He was too angry to just stand still and too angry to pace the floor.

How could he allow the same woman back into his life? Tamara was a master manipulator, willing to do anything—even sleep with him for a story.

He tried to get her to open up with him. Now he understood why she was so reluctant to discuss her past. There was nothing to tell. Tamara enjoyed playing the victim. She played well but no more.

Micah vowed from this moment forward that he would have nothing else to do with her.

He meant it this time. He was done with Tamara Hodges.

The telephone rang.

Micah checked the caller ID and saw that it was Sunni calling.

He was not in the right frame of mind to deal with Sunni and her pathetic attempt at manipulation. Unlike Tamara, she wasn't very skilled at it.

He spent most of his day outside by the pool, lost in thought and struggling once again to pick up the pieces of his broken heart.

Love is truly blind, Micah decided.

That was the only reason behind his falling for Tamara's antics. She was looking to further her career and it didn't seem to matter to her that she was using him to do it.

I'm a fool when it comes to Tamara.

Furious over his own weakness, Micah strode briskly across the room and went out on the patio.

It was a beautiful clear day in Los Angeles. Usually Micah enjoyed the beauty of nature, but now, he held no appreciation for anything and hadn't for weeks now.

He thought back to the promise he made Tamara's grandmother shortly before she died and felt a thread of guilt.

"I didn't lie to you, Mrs. Davis. Things changed after you left us. Tamara is not the girl we thought she was. I think she had all of us fooled," he whispered. "Your granddaughter played me big time, and despite the fact that I love her, I'm done with her for good."

The telephone rang again.

He had to admit that he was a little surprised he hadn't heard from Tamara by now. He half expected her to call and plead for the interview—especially since that's all she wanted from him.

It was clear to Micah that Tamara wanted her career more than anything else—even more than she wanted him.

Tamara decided she needed some girlfriend time so she called Kyra and invited her to see a movie. After they agreed on a time for the next day, she hung up.

Each time Micah tried to force his way into her thoughts, Tamara pushed him into the far recesses of her mind. She didn't want to think about the man who had used her and then tossed her out like discarded trash.

Tamara found ways to stay busy in order to get through the day without dwelling on her failed romance with Micah.

She woke up early the next morning and went to the gym to work out some of her frustration. What bothered Tamara most was that she had no idea why Micah treated her so badly.

After Tamara's kickboxing class, she felt somewhat better, but the rest of the day, she continued to battle her heartsickness over Micah.

That night when she saw Kyra in the parking lot, she waved.

They walked up to the theater together.

"How was your trip?" Kyra questioned Tamara. They had just purchased their movie tickets and were standing in line for popcorn and sodas.

Although she was dying inside, Tamara pasted a smile on her face. "It was fine. I had fun on the tour with Justice."

"I can't wait to read all about it. Actually, the reason I wanted to talk to you is because I have an idea for a story if you're interested. What do you think of writing an article about Terrence Franklin being courted to sign on as Hollington's head coach?"

"I wondered what he was going to do after retiring from the NFL," Tamara stated. "I remember how much he loved football."

"I'm hoping he will take the job." Kyra took a sip of her iced tea. "If he does, I'm definitely looking forward to next season."

Tamara agreed. "I think Terrence will make a great coach."

"It would be nice to generate as much buzz as possible."

"Can you give me his contact information? I'd like to interview him for the article."

"Now that we got that business out of the way," Kyra stated as they neared the counter, "did anything happen between you and Micah?"

Tamara tried to keep her face void of any emotion. "Nothing worth talking about," she responded.

"I'm surprised because that boy has always wanted you, Tamara. I could tell that Micah was crazy about you."

Well things have changed, she thought to herself. *He hates me now.*

Kyra ordered small popcorn and a soda while Tamara

ordered a root beer. She wasn't hungry so she decided against the popcorn.

Truth be told, she really was not in the mood for a movie, but Tamara decided that she needed to get out of the house.

Three hours later, she was grateful to be back at home. The chick flick only served to sink her deeper into depression. It was a beautiful romantic comedy, only she couldn't fully appreciate the story because of her own lack of a love life.

She just couldn't seem to get it right.

Tamara stared at the phone. She struggled with whether or not to call

Micah. It did not take her long to decide that calling him would be fruitless. The man wanted nothing more to do with her. He'd made love to her and then tossed her out. That spoke volumes.

She removed her clothes and padded barefoot into the bathroom. Tamara turned on the shower.

As soon as Tamara felt the soothing hot water on her skin, she allowed her tears to flow. She stayed in the shower until she was all cried out.

Tamara dried off and slipped on a pair of silk pajamas. She sat down on the edge of her bed and opened her journal.

September 10

I thought about calling Micah today just to get some clarity on what transpired between us, but I really don't know what to say to him. Besides, I'm not sure that he will even take my calls. He certainly hasn't tried to reach me at all. I had hoped that once I was gone, Micah would miss me or feel bad over the way he threw me out of his house and that he would call to apologize.

I chose to think that he's angry with me because the other alternative is that Micah wanted to pay me back for what happened in college. I find it hard to think of him being so cruel.

During the tour, I thought we had gotten closer and that we had truly laid the past to rest. Still, I'm left with the question of why he has such a low opinion of me. Why would he think that I'd try to manipulate him in some way just to get a story?

I try not to think that Micah used me for sex because it would hurt too much. I don't want to think of him in that way. Feeling used in that way is such an ugly emotion.

I'm not going to keep dwelling on this. If Micah wanted nothing to do with me, so be it. I don't want drama in my life.

I am going to finish my story and then forget that I ever knew Micah Ross.

Tamara closed her journal with a soft sigh.
If only it were that easy.

Micah sat at the piano in his music room.
His fingers danced over the keys, creating a mournful piece that captured his mood perfectly. He played, stopping every now and then to record the notes on a piece of paper. Some of his best songs were born out of his pain.

He had no idea of time. Micah was engrossed in his song. It pulled him along with its steady, jazzy melody.

He continued to play, wrapped up in the music, the notes embracing him like a cocoon.

Micah's fingers struck the keys until his long fingers ached.

He stopped playing and just sat there, staring off into space. Micah turned around on the wooden bench, his eyes bouncing around the room. He had a twelve thousand square foot house, more money than he could ever spend in his lifetime, a very successful company and no one special to share them with—it did not seem to make much sense to Micah.

He got up, ventured into the kitchen and poured himself a glass of wine.

Micah took it with him upstairs to his bedroom.

Although he didn't want to see Tamara ever again, he couldn't deny that her absence left an extraordinary void in his life.

He sipped his wine; the golden liquid ignited a drowsy warmth deep in the pit of his stomach. Micah sat down on one of the chairs in the sitting room, enjoying his drink.

The clock read 11:41 p.m.

Micah was tired but he wasn't sleepy. He had to fly to New York the next day for business. Since his flight did not leave until six, Micah put off packing until the next morning.

He drank the last of his wine and then stretched out on the sofa. Micah had a hard time keeping his eyes open.

His last waking thought before he drifted into sleep was of Tamara. He hated himself for his inability to stop loving her.

Chapter 11

Tamara reluctantly met her mother for a day of shopping on Saturday. She had planned to just stay home and relax, but Jillian was redecorating her bedroom for the third time in less than a year and insisted on her daughter's help.

"I was beginning to think you were avoiding me," she stated as they strolled through the bedding department, looking for a new comforter. This was the third store they had gone to. Tamara was frustrated because her mother couldn't seem to make up her mind.

"Mama, I told you I was on a huge deadline." She fingered the delicate lace sewn along the edge of a bedspread. "Just because I'm home all of the time and not in an office doesn't mean that I'm not working. I don't have all day to just shop like you do."

"Maybe if you had a husband, you wouldn't have to work so hard," Jillian pointed out. "Or if you'd just take the money I've put away for you—"

"Mama, please don't start…. I love what I do and I don't mind working for a living." She prayed her mother would move on to something else. Tamara was struggling to keep her frustration out of her voice.

Jillian would not let up. "Tamara, I'm just saying that it would be nice to have someone to come home to—wouldn't you agree?"

"I'm happy with my life," Tamara stated. "I wish you would just accept me as I am."

"All I want is the best for you. Why can't you understand that? Like this money I fought so hard to get for you. After everything that's happened, you deserve every penny."

"Mama, I don't need blood money," Tamara snapped.

Jillian's face paled. "I made sure you had a good college education and I secured your future. That money belongs to you, Tamara. Lucas Devane was a horrible husband and worse as a father. *He owes you.*"

"Mama, please be honest with me for once," Tamara implored her. "You're the one who didn't want to work or give up a life of luxury. You didn't do this for me and Callie. It was all about you."

"How can you say that?"

"I know what you did, Mama," Tamara stated. "I heard you that night on the telephone with him."

Jillian didn't respond immediately.

After a tense moment, she said, "I know how it must have sounded to you, but you need to understand that everything I did was for you and Callie. Do you know what this would do to your sister if she knew what happened?"

Tamara leaned forward. "I would never say anything to her, Mama," she said in a low voice. "I don't want Callie to know the kind of man her father really is. It would devastate her."

"My mother was right about him as much as I hate to say it," Jillian uttered. "She could see right through him. I was a young widow with a small child. I thought that he loved me. He did in the beginning…."

"I really don't want to talk about Lucas," Tamara stated.

"Did you ever find that necklace your grandmother gave you?" Jillian asked. "I've been meaning to ask about it, but with the wedding plans, I simply kept forgetting to mention it."

"I lost it in college, Mama. I'm never going to find it. I hate it, too. I really loved Grandmother's locket."

"I still think it's in some of your boxes. One day we should go through all of them. You need to get rid of some of that stuff. I'm taking my old bedding along with some other things to a Goodwill donation office. You should donate whatever you're not using, too."

Jillian pointed to the bed on display in front of them. "What about this one? It's gorgeous and very feminine."

"It's nice," Tamara agreed. "I could see that in your bedroom."

She wanted to do a praise dance when her mother decided to purchase the comforter set. Tamara was tired and wanted to get back home so that she could take a nap.

Jillian offered to buy her lunch, but Tamara begged off. After promising to call her mother later, she got into her car and left Sak's Fifth Avenue department store.

During the drive home, Tamara's thoughts traveled to Micah.

The article on Justice Kane was finished and e-mailed to her editor. Samantha would forward a copy on to Micah for his approval. Tamara had been tempted to send the article directly to him herself, but it felt like she was trying to force her way into his life.

As much as Tamara loved him, she did not want to be with a man who didn't want to be with her. The thought that he had used her for sex kept creeping into her mind, but Tamara fought off the belief that Micah was that type of man.

She felt like they were in some type of crazy cycle. Ten years ago, she'd mistakenly believed he would do something like that and had been wrong.

It's time to move on. I'm never going to get the answers I need because the one man who can give them to me, won't talk to me.

"This is so crazy," she whispered. "I need to get this man out of my head."

At home, Tamara curled up with a pen and her journal on her sofa in the den.

September 15

Mama drafted me to help her redecorate her bedroom. As always, our talks come down to finding a husband or accepting that blood money from Lucas Devane. I don't like losing my patience with her, but she just won't give up.

I still have not heard anything from Micah, but it's not like I seriously expected to hear from him. He's good at holding grudges real or imagined.

I thought that I would get over Micah eventually, but it has not happened yet.

I still love him as much as before. There are times when I feel nothing but anger toward him because of the way he dumped me, but then again, it doesn't really matter.

If Micah doesn't want to be with me then—I don't want to be with him either. Life is way too short to waste it. I decided a long time ago that I would enjoy whatever time I have left in this world.

I've finally put the disappointment and pain from my past behind me, and I've opened my heart to love.

I want to be happy.

That's not asking too much, is it?

Despite Sunni's constant, self-absorbed chatter, Micah could not get Tamara off his mind. He had been trying to flush her out of his system since the day he threw her out of the house.

As promised, Micah received an advance copy of the feature story Tamara wrote on Justice Kane. It would not be on the stands for another couple months. He had to admit that it was actually an excellent piece of work. Micah couldn't deny that she was a very gifted writer.

Before returning to his office, Micah decided to stop at the jewelry store to pick up a watch he had repaired. "I need to stop at Wyndham Jewelers," he announced to Sunni. "I need to pick up my watch."

"Not a problem, honey," she stated.

Sunni picked him up in her brand-new Mercedes luxury sedan. It was her gift to herself. She told him that she enjoyed being pampered, but if she couldn't get a man to buy it for her, then she would just buy it.

He supposed her comment was to be a hint for him; however, Micah chose to ignore it.

Sunni parked her car in front of the store.

While inside the store, a necklace caught Micah's attention. It looked familiar to him. He searched his memory, trying to recall where he'd seen it before.

Micah stole a peek over his shoulder where Sunni stood, checking out the engagement rings and her cell phone glued to her ear.

Micah wavered a moment, trying to comprehend what he was about to do. "Could you please box up this necklace, earrings and the matching bracelet?" he asked in a low whisper. "I'll be getting those, too."

The salesclerk eyed Sunni, smiled and nodded.

Micah could not believe what he was doing. *Why am I buying something like this for her? She doesn't deserve it.*

Micah couldn't explain his actions but for once allowed his heart to lead. Maybe it was time that he finally took action. It was time for him to just go after what he wanted—make his intentions plain and clear for the last time.

The clerk handed him the bag containing his purchases and his newly repaired watch.

"Honey, come look at this," Sunni said, gesturing for him to join her. Her excitement set off warning bells in his brain.

Micah walked over to where she was standing.

"Isn't this gorgeous?" she asked with a big grin on her face.

He glanced down at the huge diamond engagement ring she was pointing at and said, "Yeah, it's nice." Micah made sure to keep his tone noncommittal.

"It would look beautiful on my hand, don't you think?"

Micah shrugged. "I guess."

Out of the corner of his eye, he caught sight of a photographer standing outside the store.

"I need to get back to the office," Micah blurted. "We need to get going."

Sunni rolled her eyes. "I just want to try it on. It won't take long."

Micah kept his frustration to a minimum. He could see the headlines tomorrow—Micah Ross and Sunni shopping for an engagement ring.

When she saw that he was not interested in rings or her for that matter, Sunni released a long sigh and grunted, "Let's go."

The photographer outside the store began snapping pictures as soon as they walked outside. Sunni went into model mode while he kept a blank expression behind dark designer sunglasses.

Once they were in the car, she said, "Now I see why you were acting so mean in the store."

"I wasn't being mean, Sunni. I just don't want to be tomorrow's headline."

"Most people would kill for the kind of press that you get, Micah. I don't know why you get so bothered by it. None of your artists would be the people they are without the media, you know."

"I'm not saying that it doesn't help. I just don't want to be the one in the headlines. That's all."

"You need to get over yourself, Micah."

He recalled seeing her on the phone earlier and asked, "Sunni, did you call that guy to tell him that we were at Wyndham's?"

"Why would you ask me something like that?" she asked without looking in his direction.

"Because I know that you've done it before," he stated. "Sunni, I told you before to never do that when you're with me."

"I didn't call him," she said.

"Good," Micah responded. "I hope we have an understanding."

"We do."

Sunni dropped him off at the Ross Red offices and left to meet with her agent.

Micah had a strong suspicion that she had indeed given the photographer a tip as to their whereabouts. He was tired of being manipulated, and this time he was going to make sure Sunni understood or she would risk losing his friendship.

Just like Tamara.

However, he had some unfinished business with her. Micah planned to attend the college reunion in order to lay to rest his feelings for Tamara. Once he had the opportunity to say what needed to be said, Micah would be free to move on with his life.

He did not want to talk to Tamara over the phone. He'd speak his mind in person.

Tamara suddenly became dizzy and felt as if she were about to pass out while shopping for groceries. She left her items in the cart and went to sit down for a moment near the exit doors.

She glanced up at the clock. It was almost noon and Tamara skipped breakfast this morning, so she assumed that was the cause of her dizziness.

When Tamara felt strong enough to stand, she got up and walked over to the deli area. She purchased a sandwich and went back to the bench where she sat earlier.

She felt a little better after she ate.

Tamara returned to her cart, quickly scanning to see if anything was missing. Satisfied, she pulled her list out of her pocket and resumed shopping.

Her cell phone rang.

She saw that the caller was Callie.

"Hey, Sis," she said in greeting. "I guess you and Bryant have finally come up for air. I haven't talked to you in what? Three weeks or so. I guess married life is wonderful, huh?"

Callie laughed. "You should try it, Tamara. It's great!"

Tamara groaned. "You're not going to become Jillian Junior, are you?"

"No, you didn't just say that," her sister responded. "I was calling to see if you wanted to join me and Bryant for dinner tomorrow night. We can eat in or go out to a restaurant."

"That will depend on whether or not you or Bryant is cooking," Tamara replied.

"Ha-ha," Callie uttered. "Bryant can do it."

"Your husband is not going to work those long hours and then come on and cook dinner—not for me anyway. We can go out."

A wave of dizziness swept through Tamara once more.

"Callie, can I call you later?" she asked. "I'm in the

grocery store, and my signal isn't strong. I'll give you a call when I get home."

She decided to finish her shopping another day. Tamara pushed the cart to the first available cashier and paid for her items.

When Tamera made it to her car, she climbed inside and sat there as she waited for the sensation of passing out to disappear as quickly as it had come.

What is going on with me? She wondered.

Tamara prayed that it wasn't some type of virus going around. *Luster* magazine had a function on Friday night that she needed to attend, so she couldn't afford to get sick two days before.

She hadn't felt well for a few days now that she thought about it. Tamara was moody and tired a lot more than usual. She made a mental note to make an appointment with her doctor if her symptoms persisted.

Tamara met Callie and her brother-in-law at Ruth's Chris Steak House restaurant in Buckhead.

"Thanks for inviting me to tag along with you two lovebirds," she told them.

Callie gave her a hug. "Stop being so sarcastic. The only reason why you don't have a man is because you're so picky."

Tamara glanced over at Bryant. "She doesn't know what she's talking about."

They were seated immediately.

"Are you feeling okay, Sis?" Callie inquired. "You look a little pale."

"I'm fine," Tamara said. She didn't want to worry

her sister, especially if it were just a twenty-four hour type of virus.

Callie scanned her menu. "Do you know what you're getting as your entrée?" she asked Tamara.

"The petite filet with jumbo lump crab cake," Tamara replied. "What about you? What are you ordering?"

"I think I'm going to get what you're ordering. It sounds delicious. I know my husband will be getting the ribeye."

Bryant nodded in agreement. "I love my ribeyes."

The waiter arrived to take their drink orders.

While they waited for him to return, Tamara asked, "What are you guys doing this weekend?"

"We're going to Hilton Head with Daddy. He wants to spend some time with us."

At the mention of Lucas, her stomach turned and Tamara felt nauseous. She pretended to be engrossed in her menu.

"He asks about you all the time," Callie stated. "He told me that he feels bad about the divorce and everything. I really hope that one day you will be able to forgive my father for divorcing Mama."

The waiter returned, giving Tamara a reprieve. He gave them their drinks and then wrote down their order.

When he left, Tamara eyed her sister. "I hope this is not why you wanted me to meet you and Bryant for dinner. Lucas is out of my life, and that's the way I want to keep it. I know he's your father, but I want absolutely nothing to do with him." She was tired of being manipulated.

Callie looked visibly upset. "What I want is for the two of you to get along. He's my father, and you are my sister. What's wrong with me wanting unity in my family?"

"I'm not saying that there's anything wrong with that, Callie. The reality is that your father and I aren't even in each other's radar, Sis. Getting along doesn't apply to us. He's *your* father. You have the relationship with him."

"You have no idea how it makes me feel knowing that you and Mama hate my father." Callie looked like she was about to cry.

"I don't hate Lucas—I don't have any feelings about him whatsoever."

"Tamara, that's cold."

Shrugging, she uttered, "It's the truth." Tamara took a sip of her sparkling water. "Why don't we change the subject to something we can all agree on?"

Bryant reached over and took Callie by the hand. "Shall we tell your sister our news?"

Tamara piped up. "News? What news?"

"Bryant and I are having a baby," Callie announced with a grin. "We're pregnant."

"Does Mama know?" Tamara asked. Her mother was going to be thrilled to be a grandmother. She could hear Jillian now, barking orders for a baby shower.

Callie shook her head no. "We don't want to tell her until after the first trimester."

"I thought you two were going to wait a couple years," Tamara stated. "What changed your minds?"

"I wanted to start a family right away," Bryant contributed. "I'm twelve years older than your sister, and I want to be able to play with my children without arthritis and gout setting in," he added with a chuckle.

Her eyes traveled back to Callie, who said, "I'm happy about the baby."

Tamara studied her sister's face to see if she was

telling the truth. She knew that Callie was deeply in love with Bryant. She looked really happy and in love.

Their food arrived.

"Mama told me that you spent some time with Micah while you were in Los Angeles. She thinks that you're in love with him."

Why couldn't Jillian mind her own business?

"You know our mother," Tamara stated. She stuck a forkful of crabmeat into her mouth, chewing slowly.

"So you're not in love with him?" Callie inquired. "I thought he was your boyfriend in college."

Tamara met her sister's curious gaze. "We were just friends. He was my math tutor our freshman year, and we became friends after that. Callie, do me a favor and stop listening to Mama. When the time is right, I'll find my man. In the meantime, I don't need or want any help."

Tamara was getting tired of her family thinking that she needed someone in her life in order to be happy. Images of Micah drifted through her mind and filled her with certain sadness.

As they finished their meal, Tamara steered the conversation back to Callie and her baby. So far, her sister had experienced no morning sickness or any other symptoms associated with pregnancy. She actually looked radiant.

"I hope pregnancies like that are in our genes," Tamara stated. "With my luck, I'll be the one who's sick all nine months."

Callie chuckled. "Don't say that."

Tamara hoped that her mother would become so enthralled with being a grandmother that she would forget about her state of singleness.

At home, she made another entry into her journal. Tamara wrote about her feelings regarding her sister's marriage and pregnancy. She thought it was all nice and wonderful. Tamara wasn't jealous of Callie's happiness—she just wanted some of her own.

Tamara wanted a family. She wanted the house with the white picket fence and filled with love. She was beginning to tire of coming home to an empty house. Jillian would be so pleased if she knew this was how Tamara really felt.

She would probably throw a party.

Tamara chuckled a little at the thought.

The trouble with finding a husband was the fact that her heart already belonged to another man. However, that same man hated her with a passion.

Chapter 12

The week before homecoming, a trembling Tamara sat in her car for a few minutes; trying to digest the shocking news she had just received from her physician.

Despite how she and Micah had left things when she was in California, Tamara knew that she had to reach out to him once more.

She called and left a voice mail message on his cell phone. She also placed a call to his office and spoke with Bette, his secretary.

"Please call me back," she whispered. "I really need to talk to you."

The next day, there was still no word from Micah.

Tamara opted not to call him again. She had too much on her mind to have to try and chase after a man who didn't have the decency to return a simple phone call.

One thing she had learned about Micah was that the man could really hold a grudge. He could use a lesson or two on forgiveness, she thought to herself, then felt like a hypocrite. Tamara carried a load of unforgiveness in her own heart, although she kept telling herself that she had a valid reason.

In the five weeks that she had been home since that night she spent with him, Tamara felt a rush of emotions. She loved Micah, and if she could, she would be with him right now.

Tamara still held on to her questions about that morning—mainly why Micah didn't trust her anymore. They no longer mattered, she supposed. The fact remained that something happened the night before that affected and changed her life for all eternity.

As much as she wanted to do so, Tamara would never be able to forget that night she and Micah made love. It would forever be imprinted on her heart in many ways.

Dazed, she made the drive home in the midst of the distraction of traffic noises, the radio and her turbulent thoughts. Tamara had a headache and just wanted to lie down and sleep.

At home, she put on some soft jazz, made some hot tea and sat down in her den in an attempt to force her body to relax.

Tamara finished off her tea as the music playing in the background soothed her. She never made it up to her bedroom because she fell asleep on the sofa. Her last thought before Tamara closed her eyes was of Micah.

She slept for almost two hours, waking up when the telephone rang. Tamara sat up, stretched and yawned. She swung her feet off the sofa and stood up.

Tamara felt light-headed for a moment so she sat back down. She had an upset stomach to add to the dizziness. Groaning, she lay back against the plush cushions with her eyes closed.

Fifteen minutes passed.

She made a second attempt to stand up and made her way to the kitchen where Tamara prepared a pot of chicken noodle soup.

I'm not sure I can keep this down, but I need to put something in my stomach.

Tamara's eyes filled with water. She wiped her eyes with the back of her hand. "I'm not doing this," she uttered. "I can survive this. It won't be easy, but I'll manage."

Her eyes traveled to a nearby calendar.

Homecoming was next Friday. She had heard that Justice Kane was performing at the reunion dance, so Tamara was fairly sure that Micah would be in town for the weekend.

She felt a tinge of apprehension at the thought of seeing him again. Regardless, she needed one final conversation with Micah. After that, the ball was in his court and Tamara would follow his lead.

Friday, October 16

It's Friday and tonight is the cocktail party the university hosts for the largest contributors and VIP alumni. I'm going to cover the event for the magazine. I look forward to homecoming every year, but this one is special because it is my ten-year reunion.

The committee members have some events

planned to celebrate in addition to the regular homecoming activities. We have an alumni dance tomorrow night and we're having a picnic on Sunday.

As soon as Micah arrives, I am going to pull him off to the side so that we can talk. I need to know what made him so angry or if that was just part of his plan to humiliate me. I need to know so that I'll know what I need to do next.

If he wants nothing to do with me it will break my heart, but I have survived worse. I love Micah, but I refuse to make him my entire world. He and I need a real discussion because the truth is that I don't know if I can deal with his mood swings and tantrums.

I just really need to talk to Micah.

Tamara put away her journal.

She went downstairs to the kitchen to make a light lunch of tuna salad and crackers before heading back to her desk to work on the article that was due in a couple weeks.

Around two o' clock, Tamara found that she could not keep her eyes open or concentrate on her writing. She gave up and went to lie down on the sofa. Lately she found that she tired easily and needed to take naps during the day.

Tamara did not wake up until 3:30 p.m.

Nauseous and nervous over the thought of seeing Micah again, Tamara almost changed her mind about attending the private party, but if she wanted to be taken seriously as a writer she couldn't miss this opportunity.

Besides, she promised Chloe that she would write an article on the event for *Luster* magazine. Tamara wished fervently that she felt better, however.

She made her way to the master bath where she showered and flat-ironed her hair straight, bumping the ends with a large barrel curling iron. Still feeling sick to her stomach, Tamara took her time getting ready, pausing every now and then to take tiny sips of ginger ale.

Tamara chose to wear the black Carmen Marc Valvo designer lace and sequins dress with a lace bust, sequins around the empire waist that flowed into layers of pleated chiffon. Strappy high-heeled sandals with an ankle wrap, black diamond earrings, matching ring and bracelet completed the look.

She stole a peek at the clock.

It was 4:45 p.m.

The event started at six, and she did not want to be late. Tamara would be traveling in rush hour traffic. She grabbed her purse and headed out the door.

Tamara got in her car, slipped in her favorite Mary J. Blige CD and drove out to the freeway, humming to the music.

Her thoughts traveled to Micah. What if he decided not to come for homecoming after all?

A wave of apprehension washed over her as the thought tore at Tamara's insides. She hadn't really considered it until now that he could've changed his mind about coming.

What would she do then?

She didn't have an answer. If he didn't come, she still had to straighten things out with Micah and soon.

Never speaking to her again wasn't an option anymore.

* * *

Micah gave the valet his keys before strolling into CORK, a wine bar located in downtown Atlanta, with Sunni.

"Honey, I have to go to the little girls' room," she told him. "I'll be back shortly."

A couple of women recognized him and began a conversation.

"Do you remember us?" they asked in unison.

He studied their faces. "June? We had a history class together, right?"

She giggled and nodded.

Micah glanced at the other woman and said, "Your face is familiar but I'm sorry. I'm at a loss."

Her lips turned downward. "It's Christine. We didn't have any classes together, but I dated your roommate for about six months."

He remembered her then. "It's good to see you again, Christine. Have you and Ron kept in touch over the years?"

She smiled and nodded. "He and I just started seeing each other again. Ron will be in town tomorrow morning. He had a business meeting and couldn't get here in time for the reception tonight."

Sunni blew out of the bathroom as if someone was after her. She flung her hair over her shoulder as she sauntered toward Micah and the women.

"Are you ready?" she asked him before greeting the two females standing beside him.

He introduced her to the women.

When they left, Sunni asked, "So when do I get to meet some of your friends?"

"How do you know those two women weren't friends of mine?" he demanded.

She turned and surveyed his face. "You've been in a weird mood since we arrived here in Atlanta. Micah, what's going on with you?"

His mouth tightened a moment before he answered her. "I'm fine."

Micah and Sunni navigated through the wine bar. He walked up to his longtime friend, saying, "Hey, Kevin, what's up?"

The two men embraced.

Micah introduced Sunni to his friend. He was beginning to regret bringing her to Atlanta. Actually, she invited herself, and he didn't bother to talk her out of it. Sunni could be great company when she wanted to be.

She accepted a glass of wine from a passing waiter and took a sip.

"Man, it's good to see you," Kevin told him. "Thanks for bringing Justice Kane to my club tomorrow night, man."

"Hey, this is how we roll, bro," Micah stated.

Kevin nodded. "The place is gonna be jumping tomorrow night."

Micah chuckled. "I hope so."

While they talked, Sunni strolled away to pose near the bar. Micah assumed she must have spotted a photographer or TV reporter hanging around.

His eyes traveled the length of the room, searching. Turning his attention back to Kevin, he said, "Hey, I was surprised to hear that you and Chloe are dating. When did this happen?"

"We've been together for about three months and we click. What can I tell you?"

"That's great, man," Micah stated. "I'm happy for you both. She's a nice lady."

"I have something special planned for her tomorrow night," Kevin stated. "I hope you plan on sticking around for a while. How are things between you and the supermodel?" Kevin inquired, his eyes traveling over to where Sunni stood surrounded by fans and admirers.

"Kevin, she and I are just friends. I told you that."

"Man, what's wrong with you?" he wanted to know. "That woman is *fine,* and it's obvious that she loves you. What's holding you back?"

"She and I want different things out of a relationship," Micah replied. "We do have a good time together, though."

With those words, Micah's eyes surveyed the room, looking for the one person who had dominated his thoughts night and day for the past couple months.

Tamara Hodges.

Tamara made a pit stop to the restroom as soon she walked through the doors of the wine bar. She rushed into the nearest stall and emptied the contents of her stomach. When she came out, she found that she wasn't alone.

"Are you okay?"

Tamara eyed the woman's reflection in the mirror, recognizing her. "Hey, Beverly. I'm fine," she responded. "At least I will be in a few minutes."

Beverly Turner was crowned the homecoming queen their senior year in college.

"Tamara, it's so good to see you again," she stated with a sincere smile. "It's been a while, huh?"

Tamara nodded. "Time goes by so fast. You were my first interview for the *Atlanta Daily* after we graduated." Tamara worked with the newspaper for six years before leaving to write for *Luster*.

"You did a great job on the article, by the way—I don't know if I ever told you."

Tamara smiled. "You sent me a nice note thanking me. In fact, I believe I still have it."

They continued to make small talk, catching up with current events.

She soon became gripped by another bout of nausea. Tamara put a hand to her stomach and rushed back into a nearby stall. She prayed for the sensation to pass.

"Are you sure you're okay?" Beverly asked a second time when she walked out.

Nodding, Tamara responded, "My stomach is a little upset."

"I hope I'm not being too nosy, but are you expecting a baby?"

She responded by asking Beverly, "Do you have children?"

Beverly gave a slight nod, then responded in a voice filled with sadness, "One."

Noting the pain etched all over Beverly's face, she did not push her to say anything more.

"I just found out," Tamara said in answer to the question Beverly posed earlier. "I'm still reeling from the shock when I'm not hanging my head over a toilet."

They talked for a few minutes more.

"I guess we should make our grand entrance," Tamara stated.

Beverly smiled and agreed.

They did one final check in the mirror before leaving the bathroom and going their separate ways.

Tamara walked upstairs, following the music and enjoying the quiet ambiance of the bar.

Her heels tapped across the dark wood floors as she walked past the wall of wine barrels, a large mahogany bar with a backdrop of rows and rows of wine bottles and an array of hors d'oeuvres on the countertop.

A waiter approached her carrying a tray of wine.

"No, thank you," she responded.

Tamara made her way around the center of the room, pausing to chat with old friends. She eventually ventured to one of the tall tables located off to the side and sat down on a stool.

Tamara spotted Beverly Turner, the woman she had encountered in the bathroom, and wished she had gotten her contact information. Beverly designed clothes and owned a boutique. She made a mental note to get her business card before leaving. Tamara had an idea for another feature story.

Her gaze traveled to Chloe who smiled and waved. Kyra walked over to where she was sitting and said, "You look pretty, soror."

"You do, too," Tamara responded, fighting the urge to get sick again. Her nose was more sensitive than normal, and the mixture of food smells, perfumes and wine were all doing a number on her.

"Do you want a glass of wine?" Kyra asked after chatting for a few minutes.

Tamara shook her head no. "I'm strictly on ginger ale tonight. My stomach's upset." She prayed that her friend wouldn't get curious enough to start asking questions.

"I hope you feel better," Kyra told her. "Have you eaten anything? Can I get you something?"

Tamara replied, "No, thanks, soror. I'm not hungry right now."

"There's Terrence," Kyra stated. "I need to go over and talk to him for a minute."

She looked over at the former football star and gave an understanding nod. "See you later."

Tamara enjoyed the quiet elegance and the ambiance of the club's color theme of deep reds and browns.

She found it soothing until Micah's face loomed before her.

"You look like you're a million miles away. Are you finding inspiration for another story?" he asked.

"Hello to you, too," Tamara responded, becoming increasingly uneasy under his scrutiny. Awkwardly, she cleared her throat. "Micah, I'm glad to see you actually. We really need to talk."

"I came over here to tell you the same thing," he stated. "There's something I should've told you a long time ago."

Tamara flinched at the tone of his voice and stirred uneasily in her chair. "I see you brought Sunni with you. Are you sure you'll have some time to spare?" She knew that she sounded like a jealous woman, and there was no denying it.

"I'll make time."

She nodded. "Micah, I don't know what's going on with you or why you're treating me like this. I wish you'd just tell me what I did. Do you think that maybe we could go downstairs to the sitting room and talk—"

Micah cut her off by saying, "We can talk right here."

Tamara sighed in resignation. "Fine," she uttered. "I'll go first, if you don't mind. Micah, I don't want to keep you from your date so I'll make this quick. Remember the incident with the condom?"

Without waiting on a response from Micah, she announced, "I'm pregnant. I just thought you should know that you're going to be a father, and before you accuse me of trying to trap you, I don't want or need anything from you. Oh, I'm willing to take a DNA test, if you want one done."

She stood up. "That's it. I really don't feel well, so I'm leaving. Enjoy the rest of your evening and your date."

Tamara walked as fast as she could. She just wanted to get as far away from Micah as possible. She held her tears in check, refusing to let him or anyone else see how much he had hurt her.

Lifting her chin defiantly, Tamara did as she had always done. She plastered a smile on her face and pretended all was well with her world, while on the inside, her heart was breaking into a million little pieces.

Chapter 13

Micah followed Tamara, gently grabbing her arm to keep her from running off.

They stood near the bar on the main floor. Keeping his voice low, Micah told her, "Tamara, you can't just drop something like this on me and then walk away."

She folded her arms across her chest. *"Really?"* Tamara questioned. "Do you think I wanted to tell you something like this in this way? Micah, I've been trying to contact you for weeks, but you wouldn't return any of my calls or my e-mails. When I found out about the baby last week, I didn't bother because I knew that you wouldn't talk to me. And I definitely wasn't going to leave the news with your secretary. Seeing you here was my only chance."

Sunni strolled over to where they were standing.

Wrapping an arm around Micah, she met Tamara's gaze straight on and said, "Here you are, honey. I've been looking all over for you. Hello, Tamara."

"It's nice to see you again, Sunni. You look beautiful as always."

"I was about to say the same thing about you," Sunni responded with a smile. "I love your dress."

"Sunni, can you give us a moment, please?" Micah asked. "I really need to finish my conversation with Tamara."

The way that Sunni cut her eyes at him showed she was not happy about being sent away. After a long break in conversation, she responded, "I'll be at our table."

"I have to get out of here," Tamara stated. She pressed a hand to her stomach.

"Are you okay?" Micah asked out of concern.

"I'm fine," she managed. "I'm just a little nauseated."

"Why don't you sit down for a few minutes?" Micah suggested.

Tamara shook her head no. "I just want to go home. It was a bad idea for me to come in the first place. I knew that I wasn't feeling well, but I wanted to see you." She met his gaze. "To tell you about the baby. I've done that now, so I'm leaving now."

"Tamara…"

She shook her head. "I can't do this now, Micah. I really don't feel well. We can talk later…if you want to talk." She walked away from him, her heels tapping a steady rhythm across the floor.

"I assume you two have finished talking business," Sunni stated when he joined her at the table. "Is she okay?"

"Why do you ask?" Micah wanted to know.

"Tamara looked really upset about something." Sunni gave him a mischievous grin and asked, "What did you just do? Did you just break her heart?"

Micah didn't respond.

"Honey…" Sunni prompted as she surveyed his face. "Oh my… I don't know why I didn't see this before. It's *her.* She's the one."

He frowned in confusion. "What are you talking about?"

"I need you to be really honest with me right now, Micah. You're in love with Tamara, *aren't you?*"

"Sunni, we need to talk."

A flash of hurt crossed her face. "Micah, why did you bring me here? Especially when you knew that the woman you loved would be here, too. Were you trying to make Tamara jealous?"

"Sunni, it wasn't like that," Micah uttered. "Tamara and I… Let's just say that we were never meant to be, but now there is a situation." He paused a moment before continuing, "She's pregnant with my child."

Her thick, heavy lashes that shadowed her cheeks flew up. "What did you just say?"

"Tamara's carrying my child." He and Sunni were friends, and at times, she was his confidante. Micah knew that he could trust her with this secret.

"That would mean that you recently slept with her…" Sunni's voice died as the truth of her statement sunk in. Her eyes grew wet with unshed tears. "You slept with her during the tour, didn't you?"

He did not bother to answer her question. Micah didn't think he needed to confirm or deny when he and Tamara made love.

"Please don't tell me that you believe her?" She wanted to know. "How can you be so sure that the baby is yours? How do you know there really is a baby?"

"Because I know Tamara," he responded. "She's not the type of woman who would lie about something like this."

"People change," Sunni uttered. "She knows that you're a powerful and very wealthy man. You don't know what she's been doing in Atlanta."

Micah stated, "Tamara comes from an extremely well-to-do family. Believe me, she doesn't need my money."

Tears glistened in Sunni's eyes. "I can't believe this," she whispered. "I knew that she was after you. I knew it."

"This is not Tamara's fault. Sunni, I'm sorry. I just wanted to be honest with you."

"You have always made it clear that you didn't love me." Sunni gently wiped her eyes. "But I hoped that one day you would get a clue. I love you more than my own life, and I allowed myself to believe that you would eventually fall in love with me."

"I'm sorry."

"Don't be," she uttered with a shake of her head. "You never lied to me—I love you for that, Micah. We have been friends for a long time, and I hate to see that end, but I don't think I can do this anymore. I want marriage and a family."

Micah nodded in understanding.

"Before I leave, I want to offer you some advice, friend. You need to find Tamara and straighten out this stuff. You love her, and I have a feeling that she loves you, too. Work it out before your baby is born."

"Sunni, where are you going?"

"I'm going back to the house and pack. I'll stay at a hotel tonight and catch the first flight back to Los Angeles tomorrow."

"You don't have to leave the house. It's fine for you to stay."

She shook her head no. "It's best that I leave. If you're going to try and work things out with Tamara, you definitely don't need me in your house. I know if it were me, I wouldn't want her anywhere near you."

Micah embraced her. "Sunni, you deserve a man who will love you completely."

"I know that," she responded with a smile. "That's why I'm walking away instead of giving you a much-deserved beat down."

"That's right. You are a black belt in tae kwon do."

"Micah, I really wish you the best. I hope that Tamara will wake up and realize just how lucky she is, but if she doesn't call me."

"I don't know what's going to happen between me and Tamara. I'll just have to take it one day at a time."

"Micah, she loves you. I'd bet money on that. Go talk to her." She put a hand to her temple. "I need a glass— no, a bottle of very expensive champagne. Better yet, I think I need some whiskey straight."

"I will," Micah said with a chuckle. "Don't overdo it with the alcohol."

"I'll be fine."

"I need to make a few more rounds here, but as soon as I can get away, I'm going to talk to Tamara."

"You know I'm only a phone call away if you need me," Sunni stated. "I won't hold my breath though."

"I care a great deal about you," Micah confessed.

"In a best friend kind of way," she responded. "Which I hate but I'll deal with it. Tell reporter girl that she won after all."

"Sunni…"

She held up her hand to ward off his comment. "It's my last zinger, okay? Now move on, so I can scout for your potential replacement before I take off."

Micah released a short sigh of relief. It had gone better than he thought it would. He made a mental note to have Bette send Sunni some flowers on Monday.

Kevin signaled for him to join them at a nearby table. Straightening his jacket, Micah headed in their direction. He was ready to leave because he wanted to catch up with Tamara.

"Where's Sunni going?" he asked Micah.

"She's leaving shortly. She's going back to Los Angeles."

Kevin gave him a puzzled look.

"I'll explain later," Micah uttered.

An hour later, he walked out of CORK and got into his Land Rover SUV. Micah silently debated whether to call Tamara to let her know that he was coming over but decided the element of surprise was the best way to proceed in this situation. This way she could not tell him not to come.

There was an innocent child involved. He would not leave until he and Tamara laid everything on the table.

"Micah, what are you doing here?" Tamara asked when she opened her front door to find him standing outside.

She glanced around to see if Sunni was lurking somewhere outside. "Where is your date?"

"She's not with me," he said in response. "I know it's getting late but I had to come here to see you. Tamara, we need to finish our discussion. I would rather not do it out here, but I will if I have to." Micah's tone brooked no argument.

She stepped aside to let him enter into her apartment.

They sat down in the living room.

Tamara spoke first. "Micah, I don't know why you're so angry with me, but I don't really care anymore. I have a baby to think about, and if you're not ready to open up to me then just leave. I can raise my child on my own. I'm not gonna let you stress me out."

"Tamara, I didn't come to stress you out," Micah stated. "But I'm not going to let you keep me out of my child's life. I will go to court if I have to—I'm serious about this."

"Do what you feel you must," Tamara retorted. "I don't care about your threats. I've had enough threats to last me a lifetime."

Puzzled by her comment, Micah asked, "What are you talking about? Tamara, when are you going to tell me why you have this wall erected all around you? I've been thinking all along that you were nothing but a taker. You get what you need from me and then kick me to the curb, but now…I'm not so sure."

He held his hands up in resignation. "The truth is that I don't even know you anymore. There are so many conflicting things about you."

She gasped in surprise. "That's what you really think of me?" Tamara wanted to know. "Why would you think something like that?"

"You needed a tutor, and I was there for you. When you needed a friend, I was there. But then when I ask you out, you told me in no uncertain terms that I was beneath you. When we were in Los Angeles, you wanted to snag an exclusive interview with me. We made love and I thought that we had shared something really special until that next morning. The first thing you can think to say to me is to ask if we can do the interview now. How do you think that made me feel?"

"Micah, it was nothing like that," Tamara responded. "You totally misunderstood everything. I've never tried to use you. We were friends and I valued our friendship. There was a lot going on with me."

"You keep saying that," Micah retorted. "So what was it, Tamara? What was going on with you? You keep talking about this great friendship that we shared, yet you've been keeping all these secrets. Why is it I never knew that you wanted to be a writer? I feel like we were involved in two very different relationships."

Her hands twisted in her lap. "It's true that there are some things that you don't know about me. Micah, I need you to believe that the only reason I never told you is because I didn't want you to think badly of me. Something bad happened to me before we met."

Micah surveyed her face. It was something in Tamara's eyes that prompted him to say, "Please tell me what happened to you. Help me understand."

"On the outside we looked like the perfect family. Micah, my stepfather…he was an awful man to me," Tamara stated. "Lucas was nice enough when he and my mother were dating, but after they married he wanted to send me away to boarding school. My mother refused. Anyway, whenever she wasn't around, he would say hurtful things. He verbally abused me, and when I would try to stand up for myself he started hitting me and threatening me if I said anything to my mother."

"Babe, I'm so sorry," Micah murmured. "I had no idea."

"This went on for a couple years. He would always tell me that if my own father didn't love me, how could I ever expect anyone to love me? I believed him."

"Tamara..."

Her eyes filled with tears. "Please let me finish. I need to get this out."

Micah got up and crossed the room to sit beside her. He took her hand in his.

"Go on, sweetheart."

"One day, he just started being nice to me out of the blue. I think I was sixteen or seventeen at the time. He started buying me little gifts, and he acted like a dad. He even apologized for the way that he had treated me in the past—blamed it on his drinking too much and stress from company business. Sometimes he would come to my room at night and we would talk for hours."

Tears streamed down Tamara's face. "All I ever wanted him to do is love me like he loved Callie. I just wanted him to be my dad, too." She put her hands to her face and sobbed.

Micah handed her a tissue.

When she had stopped crying, he asked, "Baby, what happened? Tell me."

Tamara focused on the intricate designs of the wrought-iron fireplace screen as she talked. She was too ashamed to look directly at Micah. She didn't want to see the look of disgust on his face when he heard what happened between her and Lucas.

"I thought we were on the way to being a real family, but then one night he came to my room and started to touch me. He made me touch him in return."

The muscles around his mouth tightened, and Micah's hand curled into a fist. His heart ached for the woman he loved and the pain she was forced to endure. How could a man do something like this to a child he was supposed to protect?

Tamara wiped her face. "I wanted his love, but I never wanted him to love me in that way. That's not what I wanted from Lucas."

"Did he…" Micah couldn't even say the words.

"It only happened once," Tamara stated without emotion. "He was planning on doing it again, but when he came to my room a few nights later, my mother burst into the room just as he was removing his pants. He started blaming me, saying that I seduced him and that I'd been coming on to him for weeks."

He had never been a violent man, but he was ready to put her ex-stepfather into the grave. "Did your mother believe him?" Micah questioned. "Is that why you went to live with your grandmother?"

"To her credit, Mama didn't believe him for a minute, but it didn't stop her from using what happened to blackmail him into giving her half of his millions. She took me to a doctor and had everything documented. She knew that Lucas was deathly afraid of going to prison. We moved in with my grandmother and Mama filed for divorce. She signed a prenuptial agreement when they married but she used what happened to me to get it invalidated. She got the house, two of the cars and a hefty settlement. She and Callie moved back into the house but I couldn't— That place held so many bad memories for me. I just couldn't go back."

Tamara glanced over at him. "Micah, I never meant to hurt you. I was going through hell back then. I didn't trust anyone, especially a man. That's why I reacted the way that I did when I heard those people talking about us. As for the article, I won't lie—I really wanted the exclusive on you, but that's not why I made love to you. I've been manipulated all of my life and I hated it, so I would never try to manipulate another person, including you."

Micah felt lower than something he scraped off the bottom of his shoe. His guilt intensified when he thought of how he had treated Tamara, the woman he claimed to love. He was no better than Lucas was.

"I'm so sorry for assuming the worst, Tamara. I feel like such an idiot. I had no idea that you were dealing with something this heavy. I wish you'd felt safe enough to confide in me back then."

"There really wasn't any way that you could've known," she responded. "I was determined to keep my secret by any means necessary. It was just too shameful to tell you something like this."

"Does Callie know? I can't imagine she'd even let him near her after what he did to you."

Tamara shook her head no. "He gave Mama everything she wanted on the condition that she and I never mention what happened to my sister. He loves his daughter and doesn't want her to think badly of him.

Callie adores Lucas, and they have a close relationship."

"How do you feel about what your mother did?" he asked. "I know things were pretty intense between you two in college."

"Back then, we didn't really get along at all," Tamara admitted. "I blamed her for using what happened as a threat in the divorce. She didn't want to go back to being poor so she used blackmail to keep her social standing in the community and her lifestyle. I don't care about all of that—he should have paid for what he did to me."

"Tamara, she didn't blackmail him," Micah interjected. "I think you mother was making sure that she received what was rightly hers. I think she deserved it all. I do agree with you that your stepfather should have gone to jail. But what would you have said to Callie?"

"That's why I never pressed charges," Tamara told him. "Part of their agreement was that Lucas had to undergo therapy, and he wasn't allowed to see Callie without supervision until she was sixteen. He was furious about that. Mama even insisted that Callie study karate in the event she needed to protect herself."

"Didn't you study, as well?" Micah asked.

She nodded. "It was too late for me. My virginity, my dignity and my security had already been taken away."

He wrapped his arms around her, wanting to offer her some comfort.

"As for the writing, I didn't have a lot of confidence in my ability so I never talked about it. I felt that if I didn't mention it no one would ask to read my work. Working at the *Atlanta Daily* helped me develop my skills. Now you know all of my secrets, Micah. You can leave if you want to. I won't fight you on visitation. I don't need your money, though."

"I fully intend on supporting my child, and I want you to understand something, Tamara. I'm not going anywhere. I intend to be a very active parent in my child's life. Now, if you're done talking, it's my turn to speak," Micah stated. "I have something I need to say to you."

It was time for him to come clean with her about everything. When Micah was done, there would be no more secrets between them. Everything would be out in the open—the way it should have been all those years ago.

"Micah, before you say anything more, I need to make this clear to you. I don't want you hanging around because of the baby or because you feel sorry for me."

"Why would I feel sorry for you?" Micah asked. "Tamara, I happen to think that you're the bravest person I know. Not many people could have gone through something like that and be the person that you are now. Even back then, you were always smiling. None of us had a clue that anything was wrong."

Tamara met his gaze straight on. "I'm not sure I understand. How was I brave? I let my mother convince me not to press charges or go to the police. She told the doctor that I had been raped, but she didn't tell him that it was Lucas. There's no bravery in that."

"Yes, there is," Micah countered. "You silently carried the weight of your stepfather's abuse to protect your sister all these years. You're still protecting her from the truth. Callie has no idea what kind of man her father really is and that's thanks to you. Lucas is afraid of you, Tamara, because you hold all the cards. One word from you and he could lose his daughter."

"I used to worry every time she would go over to visit him," Tamara confessed. "I was afraid he would do the same thing to her."

"Are you sure that he hasn't?"

Tamara nodded. "Callie would have fallen apart. That's not something she would be able to deal with. I just found out last week that she's going to have a baby." She glanced up at Micah. "I just pray this baby is a boy. He didn't touch Callie, but I don't know about a grandchild. I couldn't be quiet about this if I thought my niece was in danger."

"He should have gone to prison," Micah uttered. "Sweetheart, you have a quiet strength— I've always said that about you. It's one of the things that I love about you. Life can get crazy at times but during those times, you can't crumble. You have to stay strong."

"It's not an easy task," Tamara confessed. "I have just never been one to give up, but I will tell you that. I'm tired, Micah. That is one of the reasons I'm alone and not in a relationship. I just don't have time for drama." She put her hands to her face. "I'm really tired emotionally."

"I'm sure I added to the stress and for that, I'm sorry," Micah told her. "Honey, you don't have to face all of this alone anymore. I'm here for you. Tamara, you can tell me anything. I want you to know that."

A tear rolled down her cheek. "Right now, I just want you to hold me, please."

Micah wrapped an arm around her. "I am really sorry

about the way I've been acting. I had no idea that you had this kind of chaos in your life."

"There wasn't any way that you could have known, Micah. I wouldn't let you see my pain. Then we both just assumed the worst about the other when it came to our hearts. I'm not saying it's a good thing. We're just scared of getting hurt."

"I did the same thing to you that I accused you of—that's not cool."

"Micah, I don't hold it against you," Tamara assured him. "I just didn't know what I'd done wrong. I had no idea what upset you at the time, but I do see your point, and if it were me, I would probably have felt the same way."

"Well now that we've gotten all of this out—it's time for us to bury the past and look to the future, so I think we need to talk about the baby. Tamara, are you absolutely sure you're pregnant?"

Tamara looked him straight in the eye because she had nothing to hide. "I went to the doctor, and he confirmed it last week, Micah. I went in because I thought I had a virus but found out that it was a baby."

"I'm confused. I know we had the issue with the condom breaking the night we made love," he stated. "I thought you told me that you were on the pill or did I misunderstand?"

"I was on the pill, Micah." Tamara replied.

"Then how did this happen?" he asked.

"A few months ago, I had to get a lower dosage than what I was using before. I guess in my case, they weren't a strong enough dosage. I started having a reaction to the ones I was taking."

Micah agreed. "I take it that you're going to keep the baby."

"Of course," Tamara responded. "There aren't any other options as far as I'm concerned."

Micah held up his hands in defense. "Hey, don't hit me…. I had to ask— No more assumptions, right?"

"Right," Tamara agreed. "We're not making any assumptions. We didn't plan to conceive a child and I know this is as much a shock to you as it was to me. I also know that we're not a couple, which is why I won't force you to play a role in—"

Micah cut her off by saying, "I intend to be a part of my child's life. I want to make sure that you're hearing me on this, Tamara. You're right that we didn't plan to have baby, but we did create one and I'm not going to run away from the situation. I'm not that kind of man."

"I never thought that you were, Micah. That's why I wanted you to know that you had a child and to give you the option of being in his or her life. Like you, I didn't grow up with a father, so I would really like for this baby to have two parents." She yawned. "I'm sorry. I get tired pretty quickly these days."

Tamara glanced over at the clock on the mantel of the fireplace. "We can talk some more tomorrow because I'm sure Sunni must be wondering when you're coming home."

Micah shook his head. "Sunni's going back to Los Angeles tomorrow. I told her about the baby. I needed to make her know that there's no future for us. There never was."

"How did she take it?"

"Pretty good, I thought," Micah responded. "She

knew it all along that there was only one woman for me."

She glanced up at him. "What are you saying? I know that you've been wanting to tell me something and I've cut you off. What is it that you want to tell me?"

Micah took her hand in his. "I want you to know that I care a great deal for you, Tamara. I tried ten years ago to let you know how I felt about you. You shot me down and as much as I wanted to forget you I couldn't."

Tamara's eyes never left his face. "Micah, what exactly are you telling me?" she asked.

"That what I feel for you is much more than friendship," Micah confessed. "It goes much deeper than that. Tamara, I love you. I always have."

Her eyes filled with tears as she smiled. "Micah, I love you, too. I can't believe that we've wasted so much time."

He kissed her. "Well, we're here now, so let's not waste another minute more."

Micah lay in bed beside Tamara, propped up on his arm as he watched her sleep. Stunned by Tamara's revelation, he felt the urge to protect her. He prayed he was never in the same location as Lucas Devane. Micah wasn't sure how he would react.

He couldn't imagine how hard it was for Tamara to keep such a dark secret from him and the rest of her friends. Having learned all this, Micah better understood why she reacted the way that she did graduation night. Any woman fighting inner demons, such as what she lived with, would respond the same way.

Micah was still stunned over how well Tamara was able to hide this from him. He had always assumed she was a happy-go-lucky girl with this sunny personality; all the while she was suffering in silence.

"I won't let anyone hurt you ever again," he whispered. "I will protect you and our child with my life. I promise you, sweetheart. I'm going to keep you safe."

She moaned softly and turned over to her side.

Micah eased out of bed and walked over to the window, staring out at the heavens. Atlanta nights were always a vision of beauty, but this night seemed especially beautiful. The stars painted across the heavens and the moon seemed brighter than usual.

I'm going to be a father.

He and Tamara were going to have a child together. The thought thrilled Micah to no end. He had loved her all of his adult life, and the fact that they now shared a child that bonded them forever.

Micah wasn't complaining. He had always desired something permanent between them. If it had been up to him, he and Tamara would have gotten married years ago. He had always known that she was his soul mate.

His heart raced as he recalled her declaration of love. Tamara loved him in return. It surprised him to find out that she had loved him for as long as he loved her. Too many years were spent in misunderstandings and wrong assumptions. Micah didn't want to waste another precious minute. He and Tamara would talk tomorrow about their future to make sure that they were on the same page.

I'm not going to lose her again.

Chapter 14

Saturday, October 17

Tamara woke up to the mouthwatering aroma of sausages cooking. Yawning, she climbed out of bed and padded barefoot into the bathroom to take a quick shower.

Fifteen minutes later, she walked out wrapped in a towel.

Humming softly, Tamara slipped on her robe and headed downstairs to the kitchen.

"Good morning," Micah said when he saw her standing in the doorway. "I hope you don't mind that I made breakfast. How are you feeling?"

Tamara smiled as she sat down in one of the chairs at the breakfast bar. "I'm fine in the mornings. I don't get nauseated until the afternoon or in the evening."

Micah's presence in her home gave her great joy. This was a dream come true for her.

"Since when did you start cooking?" she asked.

He gave a short laugh. "I had to learn if I wanted to eat. Did you think that I ate out all the time?"

Micah handed her a glass of orange juice.

"Thanks," she murmured.

Tamara took a sip before saying, "I thought that maybe you had a chef on staff or something."

He shook his head. "No, I do my own cooking."

"Do you need any help?" she asked.

Micah shook his head no. "I have everything under control. You just sit there and look beautiful."

She talked to him while he finished cooking.

Micah fixed their plates and placed them on the breakfast bar. He came around and sat down beside her.

"Tamara, you know that my mom was a single parent," Micah stated after blessing the food. "It wasn't easy for us, but we managed to have a good life. I know that this is a really confusing time for both of us and with our penchant for misunderstandings, I want it to be clear to you that I don't want that for my child. I'm not talking about the money aspect of it—I missed out on having a father. That's what I wanted most."

"Micah, I already told you that I won't keep you away from your child," Tamara said. "I mean that. If it'll make you feel better, we can have some type of legal document drawn up for visitation."

He met her gaze straight on. "Sweetheart, what I'm trying to tell you is that I don't want to be a part-time father, either."

She lay down her fork and wiped her mouth on the edge of her napkin. "Micah, what exactly are you saying?"

"I've always been crazy about you, Tamara. Now that I know you love me as much as I love you, I'm saying that I want you to be in my life. We made love last night—it wasn't two people having sex."

Micah sliced off a piece of sausage with his fork and stuck it in his mouth. "I have always wanted to be in a committed relationship with you."

Tamara finished off her scrambled eggs. "I don't want to rush into a relationship just because I'm carrying your child, Micah."

"That's not what this is," he responded. "Tamara, we've known each other for fourteen years, remember? Look, if you're not interested in—"

"That's not it at all," she quickly interjected. "It sounds to me like we want the same things, Micah. I definitely want you in my life and not as just my friend. I want a relationship with you but we have to consider the fact that you live on the West Coast and I'm here in Atlanta. All I'm saying is that there's a lot to talk about— like if you're moving here or if I'll be moving to L.A."

"You're right," Micah stated. "I know that we won't be able to figure it all out this weekend, but we have to start somewhere. Right now all I want to do is pamper the woman carrying my unborn child. Now that I've fed you, I want you to go upstairs and get back into bed. We've got a lot going on today, but before that, I have some people coming over."

Tamara reached for the jar of apple jelly. She loved putting some on her toast and was touched that Micah remembered. "What people? Who's coming to the house?"

"Relax, sweetheart," he told her with a small chuckle. "I have a massage scheduled for you. You're going to get a manicure and pedicure, facial—whatever you want. Oh and a hairstylist will be here, as well."

"You don't have to do this, Micah. I don't need to be pampered."

"Yeah, you do," he countered. "You deserve to be treated like a queen. As long as we're together, I intend to spoil you and our child."

Tamara reached over and took him by the hand. "Micah, all I want is your love. I don't need anything else. Love is all I've ever wanted—not money, material stuff or anything like that. *I only want your love.*"

The telephone rang.

"It's my mother," she announced, glancing over at the caller ID. "I'll call her back later."

Micah leaned over and kissed her. "You have to forgive your mother, sweetheart. I know that you find her motives suspect, but I believe she was well intentioned. She only wanted to secure you and your sister's future."

Tamara nodded and replied, "I know you're right about the forgiveness part, but I'm just not as sure as you are about my mother's motives."

"Look at how much time we missed because of our assumptions," Micah pointed out. "Talk to your mother and really listen to her without judgment. Listen to her heart. That's where we went wrong in the first place."

"Micah, I'll think about what you've said," she responded.

He sent her upstairs to wait for the massage therapist to arrive and set up.

* * *

Tamara felt like a new woman.

The therapist used a floor cushion and utilized foot pressure and techniques along the musculature of Tamara's body. She felt a total release as tension left her body.

"This was a wonderful idea. They also have prenatal massages. I'm going to schedule some, but I have to wait until after my first trimester," she told Micah afterward. "Thank you."

He smiled. "You're glowing."

She hugged him. "That's because I'm deliriously happy. I never thought I would ever be this happy. I love you, Micah."

He reached out and took her face in his hand. "I love you, too, sweetheart."

Tamara's eyes brimmed with tears of happiness. She would never tire of hearing him say those words or the little catch in his voice as he said them.

Without another word spoken between them, Micah picked her up and carried her up the stairs to the bedroom.

"We need to get ready," Tamara reminded him as he sat her down gently on the bed.

Micah shrugged. "It's a tailgate party. We'll be fine."

He untied her robe as he told her, "You are my dream come true, Tamara."

They kissed.

She eased under the covers and watched him as he undressed.

Micah joined her in bed and pulled her into his arms. "Sweetheart, are you sure you're feeling up to this?"

She nodded. "I want you, Micah Ross."

His hands explored the soft lines of her back, her waist and her hips searing a path of desire through her. Tamara surrendered blissfully to the deep feelings drawing them together.

Micah kissed her repeatedly, courting her senses with sweet and fiery sensations. Tamara matched him kiss for kiss. His love-filled gaze traveled over her curves. She was so exquisite and sexy that Micah shivered with passion for her.

His lips seared hers aggressively as he pulled her closer to him. Tamara clutched him tightly because she never wanted to let him go.

Together, they rode the waves of passion, crying out their pleasure when their desire peaked out of control.

When their pulses returned to normal, Micah and Tamara spent a few moments cuddling before getting up and showering together.

He was dressed and ready before her, so Micah went downstairs to make some phone calls.

Tamara dressed in a pair of skinny jeans with matching jacket. She paired the outfit with a white lace shirt. She fingered through her hair and then paused briefly to place a hand to her belly where the child she created with Micah was growing.

After all these years, she and Micah were finally together. Tamara could hardly contain her joy.

"Are you almost ready?" Micah shouted, his voice carrying through the apartment.

"I'll be right there," she stated.

When Tamara came down, she found Micah sitting in the living room giving instructions to Bette.

"Schedule a meeting for me here in Atlanta," he stated. "I'll extend my stay here for a few more days."

Micah glanced over at her and winked.

Tamara walked over to a nearby mirror to give her look one final perusal.

"You look beautiful," he said from behind her.

She turned around. "Mr. Ross, you don't look too shabby yourself." Tamara liked the jeans and crisp linen shirt he wore.

An hour later, they were ready to leave the townhouse.

"I told you that we were fine on time," Micah stated as he opened the passenger door to his Mercedes luxury sedan for her. He had her pack an overnight bag because she would be spending the rest of the weekend with Micah at his home in Buckhead.

Micah stopped at a nearby grocery store so that they could pick up hot dogs, buns and sodas for the tailgate party.

Back in the car, Micah reached over and took her hand in his. "I really love you, and I'm happy about the baby. The timing is off, but I already love this child."

"I had just found out that Callie's pregnant the week before. You can imagine my shock when I found out that I was having a baby, too," Tamara commented. "I kept telling my doctor that it was a mistake. He explained that most likely my dosage was much too low. I had to get them changed because the side effects were awful."

"Tamara, I'd like for you to be honest with me about this. How do you really feel about being pregnant with my child?" Micah asked.

"I would've liked to have been married first," she

admitted. "But, Micah, I want this child, and I'm glad that you want him or her, too. I guess the big question is how we're going to raise the baby together. We haven't really discussed it."

"We've had ten years to make up for," Micah responded. "Tamara, I'm not trying to avoid the issue or anything. I just don't want to overwhelm you. We love each other. All I know is that we are going to work this out."

When they pulled into the parking lot located north of Hollington College, Micah commented, "The stadium looks nice. Too bad we didn't have it when we were here in school. Cushioned seats and backrests in the VIP section—nice."

"It's very nice," Tamara agreed.

Micah smiled. "I flew down last year for homecoming. I thought I'd see you there."

"I didn't go because I was sick that weekend. I've only missed two homecoming games since we've been out of school. It's the one game I don't like to miss."

"I need to get a sweatshirt," Micah stated. "I bought one last year, but I have no idea what happened to it."

"I have a couple, but they're packed up somewhere," Tamara announced. "I looked last weekend for them."

"How long have you lived in your apartment?"

"Almost six months. I haven't finished unpacking because I've been so busy with writing assignments, and I mentor a group of girls at church. I'm not complaining though."

"How do you like working with the girls?" Micah asked.

"I love it," she responded. "These girls need to know

that someone cares—that they are loved. Most of them don't have fathers in the home. A couple did but were going through the same thing I went through. I've been able to heal by helping them."

He wrapped his arms around her.

Kyra walked by them and then backed up, grinning from ear to ear.

Tamara smiled. "Hey, soror."

"Wow," she murmured. "It's good to see you two together like this, but I'm a little confused. When did all this happen?"

"It doesn't matter," Micah stated with a chuckle. "As far as I'm concerned, it's about time."

He kissed her.

Kevin gave him a thumbs-up as they walked over to the area where the rest of their class members gathered.

Tamara caught sight of Beverly and waved. She sat down with a few of her sorors while Micah took the hot dogs to the men standing around the grill. He stood with them for a moment to chat.

She could feel the eyes of everyone on them when Micah joined her, but she didn't care. Tamara was with the love of her life and that's all that mattered for now, other than Hollington winning the game against the Greenville Rangers.

"I am so ready for this game," Tamara stated when he sat down beside her.

"You still love football?" Micah asked as he handed her a plate containing a hamburger and chips.

"You know it."

"Got any favorite NFL teams?" Micah inquired. "I hope the Falcons aren't one of them."

"I love my Atlanta Falcons. I like New Orleans Saints, the Panthers and the New England Patriots." Tamara bit into her burger. "What about you?"

"I like the ones you mentioned, but I'm a big Dallas fan."

Tamara shook her head. "Ooh, not me."

Micah took a long sip of his drink. "So what do you think of our team this year?"

"They had a pretty good season so far," Tamara stated. "I think Terrence Franklin as head coach will be a good move on Hollington's part. Everyone really wanted to see Coach Neal succeed but emotion wears off. Football isn't an easy game—it's like construction work. Those boys have to put in work to get this done, and they need a more hands-on coach. A lot of the talk about the game today surfaced around the offense, but during the last game, the Lions defense staged a stellar goal line stance late in the fourth quarter for a 14–8 win."

Micah broke into a smile. "Have you considered a career in sports journalism?"

She nodded. "I thought about it, but I like what I'm doing much better. I'm not sure I could always be objective."

Tamara bobbed her head to the music playing in the background. "Do you remember this song?" she asked Micah.

He grinned. "I sure do. I sang it in the talent show my junior year."

"And you won first place." She took a sip of her soda. "I love to hear you sing. You have a very sexy voice."

He grinned. "You think so?"

She nodded. "I do, so I expect you to sing to our baby all the time," she whispered.

After they finished eating, Micah and Tamara went into the stadium to claim their seats.

As soon as the game started, Tamara was on her feet, cheering on the Lions.

When she sat back down, she told Micah, "I have a good feeling about this game. I really believe that we're going to win."

"The Rangers have a pretty good team this year," he told her.

"So do we," Tamara countered. "I'm telling you the truth—the Lions are going to walk all over the Rangers this day. If you don't believe that, then maybe you need to sit over there."

"Baby, you're fired up, huh?"

"Don't mess with the Lions," she uttered. "You know how I feel about my team."

Micah laughed.

The first two quarters flew by, and it was time for the halftime show. The Marching Lions put on a stellar performance, playing musical hits from the mid-to-late nineties.

Micah and Tamara stood up and began dancing to the music along with several of the alumni.

In the third quarter, the Rangers scored their first touchdown. Two plays later, the Lions scored on a four-yard touchdown.

A Ranger fumble gave the Lions the ball at their forty-two but were successful in stopping the senior linebacker from Hollington for a two-yard loss.

The Lions ended up with a 27–11 win over the Greenville Rangers.

Tamara jumped up and down, squealing with delight.

Micah smiled to himself as he watched the mother of his unborn child enjoying herself. Her love for football still rivaled his love for sports. When the Lions scored that final touchdown, he had never heard Tamara scream so loud. She was ecstatic.

At one point, Tamara turned around to find him watching her. "What's wrong?" she asked.

"Nothing," Micah uttered. "I was just thinking of how much you love this game. I'm glad we won't have to fight over the remote on game days."

Tamara laughed. "We definitely won't have to worry about that," she stated.

Micah surprised himself when he kissed her.

"Wow," she murmured. "You're not one for public displays of affection. I guess you must really love me."

"I do," he whispered in her ear. "I love you more than I love my own life. I have always loved you."

"It never should've taken us this long to get together," Tamara stated. "I've loved you for a long time, too."

"Maybe we just weren't ready," Micah commented.

Tamara stifled a yawn.

"Are you tired?" Micah asked.

"Getting there," Tamara replied. "I've gotten used to taking a nap every day."

Micah rose to his feet. "Let's get out of here. We'll go to my place so that you can get your nap in before the dance tonight."

"I thought you wanted to spend some time with

Kevin and Chloe," she pointed out. "Micah, you really don't have to stay home and babysit me. Go on with your friends and enjoy yourself. You haven't seen most of them in years."

"I'll be fine," he replied. "It's more important to me that you get some rest."

Hand in hand, they made their way out of the stadium, caught up in the crowd of students, alumni and others in attendance.

Tamara fell asleep in the car during the ride back to Micah's house.

"Wake up, sleepyhead," he whispered.

She awoke with a start.

"I'm so sorry," Tamara mumbled. "I really didn't mean to fall asleep in the car."

"It's fine. Why don't you go on upstairs and lie down for a while," he suggested when they entered his house. "I'll give you a tour of the house after you wake up."

"Sounds good to me."

Micah led her upstairs to the master bedroom. "You can lie down in here. I'll be downstairs if you need me. You can just use the intercom."

Nodding, she sat down on the edge of the king-size bed and removed her jacket. She then kicked off her shoes.

"Would you like something to drink?" Micah offered. "There's bottled water, juice and some soda, too."

"Yes, please," she responded. "Bottled water is fine. Thanks."

Micah left the room and went down to the kitchen.

When he returned to the bedroom a few minutes later, Tamara had fallen asleep.

Pleased, he eased the double doors closed and descended the stairs. Micah navigated to his office to make a couple of phone calls.

While he was on the phone with Bette, he opened a drawer and pulled out the bag from Wyndham Jewelers.

Micah eyed his purchase and smiled.

He came up with an idea that propelled him out of his seat. He needed to run an errand before Tamara woke up. Micah scribbled a quick note and left it on the counter in the kitchen.

He grabbed his keys and headed out through the garage.

Micah left Tamara a note but he hoped to pick up one last gift and get back to the house before she even realized he was gone. He knew that deep down she still had some doubts about them, and it was his plan to erase them from her heart.

Chapter 15

It was almost seven o'clock when Tamara woke up from her nap.

Tamara assumed Micah was downstairs in his office.

Since she didn't want to disturb him, Tamara reached for the remote control and turned on the television.

As she scanned through the channels, her mind was on Micah. Tamara was deeply in love with him, but she couldn't stop from wondering if Micah truly felt the same way.

Sure, Micah had said the three words she longed to hear, but did he really love her or did he just say them out of obligation to his child?

She generally tried not to be so pessimistic, but when it came to matters of the heart, Tamara faltered.

I won't accept less than I deserve.

She would not allow herself to stay bound to a man just because she was pregnant.

Tamara felt loved by Micah; there was no denying that. However, she was now filled with the fear that this was just too good to be true. Something would go wrong, especially with her being on the East Coast and Micah on the West. Tamara didn't want to worry about women like Sunni going after her man. She wanted her pregnancy as stress-free as possible.

Now she understood why Callie wanted to wait until after her first trimester. Jillian would stress her out enough once she found out that Tamara was pregnant.

She decided not to say anything to her mother until she and Micah sorted out their relationship.

My mother and I need to work on our own relationship, as well, Tamara thought silently. *I know that I have to forgive her.*

Deep down, she knew that Jillian loved her daughters and only wanted the best that life had to offer them.

Tamara knew that her mother loved Lucas and had been hurt by his actions. In her anger, Jillian wanted to fight back in the only way that she knew how, and that's what she did.

She made sure that her daughters would never have to suffer financially. Jillian could've spent the money like it grew on trees, but she didn't. She sought out advice from professionals and invested wisely. Callie was in possession of her money while Tamara refused to have anything to do with her trust fund.

Now that she had a child on the way, Tamara reconsidered. She would have most of the money placed in trust for her children. With the other, she planned to donate to the center for sexual abuse as well as a sizable donation to her church in memory of her grandmother.

Micah peeked into the room. "I was just checking to see if you were awake."

"I am," she stated. "I was in here thinking about my mother and the money. Micah, I realized something— I could've taken the money and done something positive with it." She told him about the trust for the child and donations.

"I think that's a great idea," he told her.

"I'm going to talk to my mother on Monday. Actually, I'm going to apologize for the way I've treated her over the years and ask for her forgiveness."

"She loves you, Tamara. That much I know for sure."

"I love her, too."

"Hungry?" Micah asked.

Smiling, she nodded. "Always."

"I made scallops and pasta with a creamy garlic sauce."

Tamara climbed out of bed. "Okay, now you're just showing off, Micah. I see now that I'm going to have to enroll in a cooking class or something."

He laughed. "Don't hate...."

She stood up for a minute, her hand to her stomach. "Do you have any crackers instead?"

Micah was instantly by her side. "You okay?"

"I'm nauseated." She groaned as she sank down into a nearby chair. "You made one of my favorite meals, too."

"I'll save it for you," Micah promised. "I think there's some soup in the pantry. I'll heat that up for you."

"You're being so good to me." Tamara was touched by Micah's obvious concern for her. He made her feel loved until he said, "You're the mother of my child."

Her insecurities rose as Tamara began to suspect that he was acting this way because of the baby. Hurt, she looked away from him and said, "I'm not real hungry right now."

"Maybe you should lie back down," he suggested.

Tamara shook her head no. "I need to start getting ready for the reunion dance." She tried to keep the disappointment from her voice.

Micah was watching her. "Tamara, is something wrong?"

She pasted on a tight smile. "No. Everything is fine. I'm just waiting for the nausea to pass."

"You lie down. I'm going to grab a bite, and I'll be back up in a few minutes."

"Take your time," Tamara stated. She wanted a few minutes alone to gather her thoughts.

Despite the vomiting, Tamara was a vision of beauty when she walked out of the bedroom. She had chosen a chic drop waist dress with an ostrich feather skirt in black. She paired it with black opaque hosiery, open-toe patent leather shoes with a matching clutch purse. She undid her twists and wore her hair loose and full of waves.

He could tell that something had changed between them after they arrived at his house. Micah didn't press her because he wanted to be sensitive to the fact that she wasn't feeling well at the moment, and it was possible that she was feeling a bit moody.

The dance started at eight o'clock but Micah and

Tamara did not arrive until shortly after nine. She had another bout of nausea right before leaving the house.

Micah initially tried to convince her to stay home, but Tamara wasn't going to miss it or Justice Kane's performance.

This was around the tenth or eleventh time that he had come to Bollito, the trendy nightclub in South Atlanta owned by his best friend Kevin Stayton. The popular club was comprised of several levels housed in a large, warehouselike building.

They walked through the large double doors.

Kevin greeted him and Tamara seconds after their arrival.

They paused for a moment so that he and Kevin could discuss business. Micah liked that each level featured different colored accents on each dance floor while the club was decorated in the school colors of navy and white. Each floor was devoted to a different genre of music, making it a club that appealed to almost everyone.

Micah escorted Tamara down to the main floor where the stage was positioned against the back wall. They sat down on a plush velvet loveseat in one of the private balconies.

"This is very nice," Tamara murmured. "How many of your artists will be performing tonight?"

"Two," Micah responded. "Justice and Blue Silk are singing tonight."

He wrapped an arm around her. "How are you feeling?"

Tamara looked up at him and said, "Much better."

More of the class of 1999 arrived. She got up to chat with some of her sorors and former classmates while Micah went down to check on his performers. She seemed happy, but he couldn't escape that feeling that something was bothering her.

Micah already knew she was capable of hiding her emotions behind a smile.

He would find out what was going on with her when they returned home.

Tamara glanced over her shoulder to see if Micah had returned.

When she couldn't locate him in the growing crowd, she returned her attention to the women grouped around her.

Beverly arrived wearing a form-fitting black dress that looked stunning on her. She and Tamara embraced.

"You look absolutely beautiful," she told Tamara. "I hope that you're feeling better."

"I am," Tamara stated. "I have to tell you how much I love this dress you're wearing, Beverly."

The chatted a few minutes about fashion before Beverly moved on. Tamara waved at a couple she hadn't seen since college. It was nice to see that they were still together. She was shocked to hear that they were also proud parents of seven children.

Micah came up a few minutes later and escorted her to the dance floor. The DJ played all of her favorites. Putting a large hand to Tamara's waist, he drew her body toward him. The warmth of his muscled arms as they danced was so bracing; she felt like she was dreaming.

Being this close to Micah made Tamara weak in the knees. She couldn't remember when she'd felt this way in her thirty-two years. They danced to the next couple of songs. She couldn't remember when she'd had a such a good time.

"Did I tell you how beautiful you look?" Micah asked her.

She smiled. "I believe you did. Thank you."

The DJ slowed down the music, prompting him to pull Tamara into his arms, holding her close as they moved to the sultry rhythm.

When the music stopped, they reluctantly parted a few inches. It was time for Justice to perform so they returned to their seats.

Leaving the dance floor, Micah asked, "Would you like something to drink?"

"I'm fine," she responded.

Tamara was exhausted but didn't want to leave before Justice finished performing. She could feel the heat of Micah's gaze on her.

"We can leave if you're not feeling up to this," he whispered in her ear. "I told Justice that I might have to leave early."

"I'll be okay," she assured him. "Micah, please stop worrying about me. The baby is fine. So am I." Tamara hoped he didn't hear the thread of irritation that was in her tone. She was tired, and his constant attempt to make sure all was well really got on her nerves.

Micah must have gotten the hint, because he didn't say anything else to her during the performance.

Justice took his final bow shortly after ten o'clock. Tamara couldn't take it anymore. "I'm ready," she whispered in Micah's ear. "I'm exhausted."

While Micah and Tamara were saying their good-byes, Kevin walked onstage.

"What's going on?" she asked Micah.

He looked as puzzled as she did. "I don't know. Kevin never said anything to me... Wait a minute, he did mention something about a surprise for tonight. I think it has something to do with Chloe."

She gave him a knowing look. "We can't leave yet. I want to see this."

Tamara's eyes filled with tears at the unique and very romantic proposal from Kevin to Chloe Jackson.

When Micah wiped away her tears, she told him, "You have to excuse me. It's my hormones. They're going crazy right now."

"Let's get you home."

She nodded. "I'm so ready."

Tamara did not say a whole lot during the ride back to Micah's house. She didn't really know what to say, and Tamara didn't really want to spoil the evening by bringing up something Micah might not be ready to discuss.

However, she couldn't delay this any further. Tamara was suddenly afraid that they were moving too fast, trying to force a relationship because of her pregnancy.

She couldn't fully give Micah her heart until she knew that what they were both feeling was real.

Micah had his own surprise for Tamara waiting at the house.

"You were quiet on the way here," he began. "Tamara, I need you to talk to me, sweetheart. Tell me what's wrong, please."

"I'm confused, I think," she responded. "Micah, I know how I feel about you—there's no confusion there."

"Okay, then what is the problem?" he asked.

"I need to be absolutely sure of how you feel about *me*." Tamara took a deep breath, then released it slowly. "Micah, I need to know if you're with me because I'm having your baby or if this is something you really want. I know the sacrifices you would make for your child."

"I love you, Tamara," he told her. "I love you with my whole heart. I wouldn't tell you this if I didn't mean it." Micah raised his hands in resignation. "I don't know what else to tell you."

Tamara's eyes filled with tears. "This is a dream come true for me, Micah, but I have to be realistic. We love each other, but I just don't see how this is going to work. I know you have this house here in Atlanta, but really, how often are you in town?"

"That will change because we're together," he told her.

"How? Are you planning to move here?"

"I would," Micah replied. "If my business wasn't in Los Angeles."

Tamara twisted her hands nervously in her lap. "That's what I thought."

"What about you moving to Los Angeles?" he questioned. "You can write anywhere."

Tamara wiped her eyes with the back of her hand. She hadn't really considered that option.

"Well?" Micah prompted.

"This seems to be moving really fast, don't you think?" Tamara responded. She was feeling a bit overwhelmed. Less than a week ago, she'd discovered that she was pregnant; she and Micah weren't speaking to each other and now he wanted her to consider packing up and moving to California.

"Micah, we haven't seen each other for ten years until a few months ago and now I'm carrying your child. Then you just asked me about moving to Los Angeles."

He frowned. "Are you having second thoughts about us?"

Tamara shook her head. "I love you and I want to be with you, but I…I'm scared."

He pulled her into his arms. "Sweetheart, we don't have to rush into anything. I don't want you to feel like I'm pushing you into this."

"That's not what I'm saying," Tamara interjected. She placed her hands to her face. "Micah, I really need to clear my head. If you don't mind, could you call me a cab? I think that I really need to go home tonight."

"You can take one of the cars," he told her. "But you don't really have to leave, sweetheart. If you want, I'll sleep in one of the guest rooms."

"I think I need to go home. Micah, please don't think that I don't love you. Everything is just happening so fast, and my hormones are on overload. I just need some time alone. I hope you understand."

"I'm trying," he confessed. "Call me when you get home."

"I will." Tamara hugged him. "I'm so sorry."

"I don't want to lose you, so I have no choice but to take your lead on this."

"I do love you, Micah. I just need to try and figure all this out."

Tamara kissed him before walking out of the door.

It wasn't until she was in the car that Tamara broke

down into sobs. She wiped her face and drove away from the man she loved.

"I really want this to work out," she whispered. "Are we moving too fast? Lord, I really need You to help me out with this. Help me find the answers, please."

Chapter 16

Micah clenched his fist in frustration and shook his head as he removed his jacket. *Why can't Tamara and I get this right?* He never once doubted that they belonged together, and he refused to start now.

The thought resonated in his head. They were in love and had been for years. So what was the problem?

He removed his shirt before sinking down on the sofa to remove his shoes.

Micah believed that Tamara loved him—he could see it in her eyes. However, he also saw that she was running scared, and he was powerless to stop her. She would have to find a way to deal with her fear. All he could do was love her and only if Tamara allowed him entry into her heart.

He was about to head upstairs when he heard the

garage door go up. Curious, Micah made his way toward the door leading outside.

He cautiously reached for the handle and opened the door. Micah was surprised to find Tamara standing there.

"I couldn't figure out which key opened the door," she said sheepishly.

"I didn't think you would be coming back here tonight."

Tamara followed him into the family room. "I know that you're probably wondering if I'm losing my mind, but I'm not, Micah. It's hormones," she said with a nervous chuckle.

Micah gave an understanding nod. He did not want to say anything until he had a sense of what was going through her mind right now.

She paced back and forth. "I'm thinking much clearer now, and I know exactly what I want."

"And what is that?" he inquired.

"*I want us, Micah.* I want us and everything that means." Chewing on her bottom lip, Tamara added, "That is if you haven't changed your mind."

He pulled her into his arms, kissing her until she pleaded for him to stop. "There's something else that I need to tell you."

"I don't want to talk anymore," Micah stated, shaking his head.

"This won't take long, and I know that you'll want to hear this," she promised.

"Okay," he said. "I'm listening."

"Micah, I'm not afraid anymore," Tamara blurted. "I realized when I left here that there are only a couple of times I've truly felt safe in my life and that's when I was with Grandmother and *you*. I love you, and I want to spend the rest of my life with you even if that means I have to make this move to Los Angeles."

Micah broke into a big grin. "Really?"

She nodded.

He took her hand and led her upstairs to the master bedroom where they planned to spend the rest of their evening.

Micah held Tamara in his arms.

"That was wonderful," she murmured. "I love making love with you."

He smiled. "I'm glad to hear that."

She laughed.

Micah sat up and swung his feet out of bed. "I have a little surprise for you," he announced. "I'd planned to give it to you earlier but then you ran out on me."

"I told you it was hormones."

He padded across the room to the huge walk-in closet. Micah reached in and pulled out a gift bag.

Tamara set up in bed, pulling the covers up to cover her breasts. "What is this?" she asked when he sat down beside her.

"Open it and see," Micah responded.

Tamara pulled a medium-size fluffy, white teddy bear out of the bag.

"Micah, he's so adorable," she murmured. "I'll have to put him away for the baby." Stealing a peek over at him, she said, "I have to tell you that I'm a little disappointed. I thought this was a gift for me."

"Look closer."

She gave him a questioning look. "Huh?"

"Take another look at the bear."

Tamara stared at the stuffed animal and then she saw it.

Around the bear's neck was a beautiful necklace— its design was very close to the one she lost in college.

Tears formed in her eyes. "Micah...it looks like the one my grandmother gave me."

"I remember how upset you were when you lost it," he responded. "You used to talk about passing it on to your son or daughter one day."

"Grandmother always made me feel loved and safe. When she died, that necklace was all I had of her. Of course, it wasn't as expensive as this one, but it was like gold to me because it belonged to her. Her mother had given it to her on her wedding day. My mother eloped with my father, and when she married Lucas, she wore a Devane heirloom so Grandmother passed her necklace to me."

Tamara wiped away an escaping tear. "Thank you so much, Micah. I can't put into words how much this gift means to me." Her fingers lightly traced the locket. "This is so beautiful, and I'll cherish it forever."

"I also have these for you." Micah handed her a black velvet box.

Inside was a pair of earrings and a bracelet that matched the necklace.

"I know that necklace isn't the original one that your grandmother gave you, but you still have your memories," Micah said as he put them on her. "No one can ever take those away from you. I hope that we can make new memories to pass on to our children. I want you to feel just as loved and as safe as you felt when you were with your grandmother. I promise to protect you and our child with my life."

Tamara was choked up with emotion and couldn't talk now. Any doubts that she had about them suddenly vanished.

Micah kissed away her tears. "We are going to have a great life together."

Wiping her face with the back of her hand, Tamara nodded in agreement. "I have never been happier than I am right now."

"This is just the beginning, Tamara," Micah stated, his voice filled with emotion. "If you'll trust me with your love, I will make sure that you never regret it."

Chapter 17

Sunday, October 18

The next morning appeared much too soon for Tamara. She and Micah had been up late sealing their commitment to each other.

He was up at 6:00 a.m. as usual but did not bother to wake her until 8:00 a.m., allowing her to get as much rest as she could before they had to leave for the reunion brunch.

Micah leaned over her and whispered, "It's time to get up, sweetheart."

"Nooo," she moaned softly.

Micah suspected that Tamara was not fully awake and gave her a gentle nudge. "C'mon. You know how long it takes for you to get ready."

"Then you shouldn't keep me up so late," Tamara grumbled.

"I tried to get some sleep—you were the one with the insatiable appetite," Micah teased. "You couldn't get enough of me."

Tamara opened one eye and then the other. "I think that was the other way around."

He laughed. "Actually, it was both of us."

She crawled out of bed. "This weekend has really worn me out. It's either because I'm pregnant or I'm getting old."

Micah eyed her naked body, loving her with his eyes. "You're definitely not getting old, baby. Not from where I'm sitting."

Smiling, she stole a peek at him from over her shoulder. "You always seem to say the right things. That's one of the reasons I love you."

"What are some of the other reasons?" he asked with a seductive grin.

"Meet me in the shower," she responded. "I'll show you."

Afterward, Tamara slipped on a pair of blue jeans and a white tank top. She draped a Hollington College scarf around her neck. Tamara pulled her natural curls back into a ponytail.

They left an hour later, driving across town to the campus for the annual brunch, an event geared toward the alumni and their families, regardless of graduation year. However, the class of '99 had a designated section near the food tent.

Large tents had been erected around the center lawn known as The Square. The caterer set up a large buffet of breakfast foods as well as sandwiches and Southern specialties.

White tables and chairs were spread out around the grassy area. Some of the alumni brought their own blankets and searched for empty spaces to settle down.

Micah and Tamara found a spot near Kevin and Chloe and sat down. She congratulated them on their engagement.

Kevin smiled. "You two look real good together," he told them.

"We think so, too," Micah stated. "It took me fourteen years, but I finally got the woman of my dreams."

Tamara could not keep from yawning.

"I guess you were up late with a certain someone," Kyra whispered in her ear. "All right, soror."

Tamara could feel her face heat up. "You need to quit, Kyra."

Micah brought her a plate piled with more food than she could handle.

"Who did you make this for?" Tamara questioned.

He leaned down, close enough for her ears only and said, "You're eating for two so I figured you'd need—"

"What?" Tamara interjected. "Twice the food?"

"I'll eat what you don't," he told her, grinning. "I know how much you like to enjoy your food."

"If I eat like this the entire pregnancy, I'll be big as one of your houses." Tamara smiled up at him. "You're not going to be like this the entire time, are you?"

"Like what?" Micah asked. "Protective and caring? Yeah, I am. I'm like this about the people I love."

She resisted the urge to kiss him.

He was so good to her, and while all of this attention

got on her nerves from time to time and irritated her to no end, she was not going to complain. Tamara was looking forward to a future with Micah and their child.

The homecoming parade would begin at the college stadium, wind around the small local streets and end at the center lawn.

Tamara stood in front of Micah as they waited for the parade to start. She had always loved parades, even as a child.

Several Atlanta high-school bands, local and university clubs would also be participating. Tamara had planned to help her sorority work on the float for the parade but her bouts of nausea prevented her from doing so.

The parade began.

Former homecoming queen, Beverly Clark, rode on the class of '99 reunion float. Tamara cheered and waved as she passed by them.

Micah and Tamara stayed to see the award-winning Hollington College Marching Lions perform as the parade ended.

Micah had his arms around her with one hand resting on her belly. She leaned against him and reveled in the closeness.

"How are you holding up?" he asked.

"I'm okay," she told him.

Some of the others were going to a sports bar for drinks and fellowship, but she and Micah opted to head home. Tamara was near exhaustion although she tried to put on a brave front. She knew that Micah saw through the facade and that's why he insisted on going back to the house.

"Did I ever tell you what a great job you did on *Justice*?" he asked while walking across the parking lot to his car.

Tamara shook her head. "Did you really like it?"

"You are an amazing writer, sweetheart."

"Thank you. I love what I do, and I'm trying to learn everything I can because it's my dream to own my own magazine one day."

Micah nodded his approval. "I can see that."

"I'd still like to do a feature on you for *Luster,*" Tamara stated. "But it's totally up to you, Micah. If you're not comfortable with the idea, then I won't do it."

He gave her a big smile. "I trust you, sweetheart. We can do the article. Pitch it to Samantha, and see what she thinks."

"I can tell you right now that she is going to be thrilled. I have a feeling she's going to want you on the cover, too. We need to do this before our relationship is public record though," Tamara stated.

"I was thinking along those same lines," Micah said.

"I'll send Samantha an e-mail later on tonight. I won't let you down, Micah. And you won't ever have to worry about me discussing our relationship with anyone in the media."

Micah laughed. "Worrying about you keeping secrets is not an issue for me. I already know that you are skilled in keeping your mouth shut."

Tamara elbowed him in the arm. "I deserved it, but you do know that you're wrong for that, don't you?"

They laughed as they made their way across the stadium parking lot.

* * *

Tamara and Micah were in the car driving back to his house when she asked, "Do you mind if we make a quick stop before we go back to your place? It's not too far from here. It's the—"

"The cemetery where your grandmother's buried," Micah interjected. "Today is the eleventh anniversary of her death."

She could not contain her surprise. "Micah, I can't believe you actually remembered the day my grandmother died. Wow."

"I remember it because we were supposed to hang out together homecoming weekend, but instead we were with your family," Micah explained. "You kept trying to get me to leave but I couldn't—you were devastated by your grandmother's passing."

"I didn't want to ruin homecoming for you."

He said, "It wouldn't have been the same without you. In truth, I think that is why I didn't bother coming all these years. I enjoyed spending those times with you."

They stopped at a florist shop so that Tamara could purchase flowers to put on her grandmother's grave.

A few minutes later, they were on their way. Micah drove through the entrance and pulled into an empty space near the road that led up to where Mrs. Davis was buried.

"Do you want me to go with you?"

"I can do this," Tamara stated. "For a long time, I couldn't come out here, but I need to do this today."

She got out of the car and headed down the path to her grandmother's gravesite, the roses in her hand.

Tamara easily located the grave.

"Grandmother, I miss you so much," she stated. "A

lot has happened since I was here the last time. I'm in love, and I'm going to have a baby. You met Micah when we were in college. He was that cute lil' tutor— that's what you used to call him. Well we're together now, and I want you to know that he makes me feel safe and loved. He treats me like a queen."

"Mrs. Davis, I just wanted to tell you how much I love your granddaughter," Micah said from behind her. "She means more than anything else in this world. Tamara is the love of my life."

He dropped down beside her. "I promise to keep her and my baby safe. I told you a long time ago that I would marry Tamara, and I fully intend to keep that promise. I would've proposed already, but your grand-daughter is the one holding things up."

Stunned, Tamara glanced over at him.

"You told my grandmother that you wanted to marry me?" she asked after a moment.

He nodded. "I think she knew that I was in love with you long before I knew it myself."

Tamara grinned. "That was Grandmother. She sus-pected things weren't right at home for me, but I would never open up to her. Maybe if I had, things would've turned out differently. For so long, I felt dirty and ashamed, but my grandmother—she would always make sure I understood that I had done nothing wrong. That it wasn't my fault."

"Mrs. Davis was a wonderful lady, and I enjoyed talking to her."

"When did you and Grandmother have these discus-sions?" Tamara asked out of curiosity. "I was always around you two."

"Not always," Micah told her. "I would call her from time to time to see if she was okay or if she needed anything."

Tamara stared at him in amazement. "I never knew. Grandmother didn't tell me anything."

"It was our secret."

She folded her arms across her chest. "So you were keeping some secrets, too. I didn't think it was possible, but now I love you even more."

"Are you ready to go home?" Micah asked.

"Yes," she responded. "That's what being with you feels like to me. *Home*."

Micah helped Tamara to her feet.

"Rest in peace, Grandmother," she whispered before leaving. "You don't have to worry about me anymore. I have Micah, and he's very protective. He's going to take good care of me and the baby."

Later at home, Tamara and Micah discussed the events of homecoming while they settled in for the evening.

At one point, there was a break in their conversation. Tamara stared off into space, lost in thought.

"What are you thinking about?" he asked.

Tamara turned to face him. "I was just thinking how you changed my life the day that you came to tutor me. I don't know if I ever told you that you were a great teacher."

Micah reached for Tamara. "Now it's your turn to teach me tonight."

HOLLINGTON HOMECOMING

Where old friends reunite...
and new passions take flight.

Book #1 by Sandra Kitt
RSVP WITH LOVE
September 2009

Book #2 by Jacquelin Thomas
TEACH ME TONIGHT
October 2009

Book #3 by Pamela Yaye
PASSION OVERTIME
November 2009

Book #4 by Adrianne Byrd
TENDER TO HIS TOUCH
December 2009

Ten Years. Eight Grads. One weekend.
The homecoming of a lifetime.

KIMANI™
ROMANCE

www.kimanipress.com
www.myspace.com/kimanipress

KPHHSP

REQUEST YOUR FREE BOOKS!
2 FREE NOVELS
PLUS 2 FREE GIFTS!

KIMANI ROMANCE™

Love's ultimate destination!

15
ARABESQUE®

HELP CELEBRATE
ARABESQUE'S
15TH ANNIVERSARY!

2009 marks Arabesque's
15th anniversary!

Help us celebrate by telling us about your most special memories and moments with Arabesque books. Entries will be judged by the Arabesque Anniversary Committee based on which are the most touching and well written. Fifteen lucky winners will receive as a prize a full-grain leather duffel bag with the Arabesque anniversary logo.

VISIT **WWW.MYSPACE.COM/KIMANIPRESS**
FOR THE COMPLETE OFFICIAL RULES

KPISARACONTEST